A SEASON FOR CHANGE

BOOK #25 THE AMISH BONNET SISTERS

SAMANTHA PRICE

D1528240

CHAPTER 1

*C*herish was feeding her dog outside when she looked up and saw Ada and Samuel approaching the house in their buggy. It was so early in the morning that she was surprised to see them. Hoping Matthew would be with them, she walked over.

Ada stepped down from the buggy. Then she pulled out a box from the back.

Matthew wasn't with them. "Hello. Where's Matthew?"

"He's working at Mark's saddlery store today."

"That's right. I forgot he was doing that."

Ada smiled at the box in her hands and then looked up at Cherish. "I brought chocolate cake and those chocolate cookies you love."

That made up for Matthew not being there. "Thank you."

Ada started walking to the house. "Simon left yesterday. I suppose you know that."

"He left?"

Ada nodded.

"Left for home?" Cherish asked.

"Yes." Ada stopped walking when Levi passed them and said hello. Then he got into the buggy and left with Samuel.

Cherish just stood there, staring at Ada.

"So he didn't tell you?" Ada asked.

Cherish shook her head. "No."

"I thought you and Simon were closer than that. I must've been mistaken." Ada left her and walked into the house.

Cherish was frozen to the spot. She had hoped Simon would come and say goodbye and then they'd plan something for when she went to her farm since he lived close by. What was the point? He clearly wasn't interested. Now Ada knew it too. Cherish could see it in her eyes the way she'd stared at her just now.

Bliss came out of the house. "Hey, Cherish, *Mamm* wants to know…"

"I'll be back later. I forgot to do something." Cherish ran into the orchard and when she was far enough away from the house, she slumped to the ground and allowed some tears to escape her eyes and fall down her cheeks. She hated being weak and crying was weak, but she couldn't stop.

The orchard was so barren and lifeless in the winter. The rows of leafless, tangled branches reaching up to a cold, gray sky emanated a certain eeriness. The frozen ground also did nothing to lift her mood.

It was such a shock that Simon had left without telling her. He'd said he'd stayed longer than he had meant to and she thought that was for her. Maybe he'd stayed for some other reason. Just when she'd started to see a future for herself, she'd fallen flat on her face. Was this a sign that nothing in her life would run smoothly?

Then her mind started to wander as she looked up at the clouds. What had ever gone right for her?

Dat had died and then her oldest sister, Florence, who was like a second mother, abandoned her whole family to marry an outsider. Then she got close to Aunt Dagmar and then she died too. Cherish sobbed at all the people who'd left her. It didn't matter that *Dat* and Aunt Dagmar couldn't help dying, the pain was just the same as if they'd walked out the door and kept going.

Simon leaving without a word felt just like all the other disappointments she'd suffered.

"Cherish, what's wrong?"

Cherish scrambled to her feet, wiping her eyes when she saw Bliss had found her. She didn't want her or anyone else to see her crying on the ground. "I'm okay."

"It doesn't look like it. What's upset you?"

Cherish brushed down her dress with her hands. She trusted that she could tell Bliss the truth. After all, Bliss was no stranger to life's cruel disappointments. "I'm just upset that Simon left and he didn't even say goodbye."

Bliss produced a letter from beneath her black coat. "Maybe he did."

Cherish stared at the envelope in her stepsister's hand. It didn't even have a stamp. It simply said, 'Cherish.' "Is that from...?"

"Yes. I got it from the letter box just now. I was hoping Adam might have written a note explaining his feelings and telling me why he doesn't want anything to do with me. There was something there, but it wasn't for me and it wasn't from Adam. It has Cherish written on the front and on the back it's got Simon. He must have put it in there himself. It's not been sent through the postal service."

Cherish sniffed. "It's really from him?"

"Yes. I guess so, unless you know any other Simon?"

"I wonder why he did this." Cherish started feeling a little better. He'd left, but he was thinking about her.

"Open the letter and find out. I'll be back at the house if you want to talk."

"No, stay in case it's bad news." Cherish couldn't take her eyes off the envelope. "No, go. I'll be okay. No, stay."

Bliss smiled. "Am I going or staying?"

"You go. If it's bad news, you'll hear me screaming and you can come back."

"I've got a feeling it'll be good news."

"Really?"

Bliss nodded.

"Did you read it already?" Cherish asked.

The smile left Bliss's face. "Of course not. I'd never do anything like that."

"Okay. Sorry. I didn't mean to say you would."

Cherish watched Bliss walk away. She was sad for Bliss, how she checked the letter box, hoping to hear from Adam. It didn't make sense that Adam would leave her a note, but it seemed Bliss was grasping onto any, even the smallest, hopes.

CHAPTER 2

Once Bliss was in the distance, Cherish propped herself against a tree, opened the envelope and pulled out the letter.

Hi Cherish,

I've left as you know by now if you're reading this.

I didn't want to say goodbye, because I am awful at goodbyes.

Let me know when you're at the farm and I'll come and see you. Since it's too far to go back and forth by buggy every day, maybe I can make the journey there and stay for a couple of days. I could help out at the farm and do whatever you need me to do.

I'm glad I got to know you. It would've been nice if I could've stayed longer.

We've got a phone in our barn and I've written the number and our address at the bottom of this page.

Call me as soon as you know when you'll be at the farm.

FAITHFULLY,
Simon

ALL CHERISH'S fears had been washed away. He did like her. He even signed the note, 'faithfully.' What did that mean? It had to be good. He didn't say 'yours faithfully.' That had to mean something. Maybe it meant he'd be faithful to her and not date anyone until she moved to the farm so they could continue their relationship.

Looking down at the letter, she saw how neat his handwriting was and there were no misspelled words. He was like Malachi, her farm manager, but a better version.

She held the letter to her heart. He'd given her his number and his address. Could this be the man she'd eventually marry? She'd never given much thought to the kind of man she wanted, but Simon seemed very nice. Besides that, he didn't live far from the farm she'd inherited from Aunt Dagmar. It was totally perfect.

Cherish decided to share her news with one person. That was Bliss. It would cheer her up. Cherish walked back to the house, feeling a whole lot better.

She opened the back door and then walked through to the kitchen looking for Bliss. *Mamm* and Ada were the only ones there.

Mamm glared at Cherish. "Well, where is it?"

"What?" Cherish asked.

"I sent Bliss out to find you to ask where you put the cookie jar."

"It's on the top shelf."

"What's that you've got there?" With one swoop, *Mamm* stretched out her arm and plucked the letter out of her hands.

"Nee, Mamm. That's private."

Mamm turned the envelope over, looking at the back and the front. "While you're under my roof, nothing is private."

"That's right, Wilma. That's what I used to tell my *kinner."* Ada chortled.

"And that's probably why they moved out," Cherish quipped, as she made a grab for the envelope while *Mamm* held it out of reach.

"I think you were rude just now, Cherish," Ada sneered. "My children moved out when they married and not before."

"Sorry. I know I was rude." It was easier to admit it and agree with Ada. She'd learned that the hard way. Finally out of exasperation, Cherish told her mother, "It's from Simon."

"I can see that. So what's he got to say that I can't see, hmm?"

"Nothing."

Mamm said, "I'm reading it, so sit down while I have a look at what he's saying to my youngest daughter who is not of marrying age. I thought he seemed too keen to spend time with you. I didn't like it when he asked if he could go for a walk with you after dinner the other night."

"I thought you liked him, Wilma," Ada said.

"I do as a person, but I didn't like it when he asked in front of everyone if he and Cherish could walk outside— alone. He did that deliberately so Levi and I wouldn't say no. It was too cold out, and a storm was brewing so his decision wasn't wise. They would've been better to talk on the porch, but oh no. He knew best. Now sit down, Cherish, while I read this."

Ada sipped on her cup of hot tea while Cherish sat down. "Sure, *Mamm*, read it, but I will be old enough to marry soon. And I can even marry now with your permission."

Mamm made a mocking sound from the back of her throat. It was a cross between a laugh and a croak. "Permission? You won't get that. You'll marry when you're mature enough and not before. For some, that's eighteen and for some it could be twenty-eight. I'd say you'd fall in the group who will marry at twenty-eight." *Mamm* pulled the letter out of the envelope.

"What happened to mail being private?" Cherish grumbled.

"Oh, you can have private mail when you're no longer living in this house under my roof."

Ada smiled. "You tell her, Wilma."

Cherish suddenly thought of something. As per the agreement after they found her father's will, the orchard belonged to the shareholders. And just like that, Cherish realized that she was more of an owner of this house than her mother was. But, she'd get nowhere pointing that out and could very well get sent to her room. Or worse, she wouldn't get to visit the farm for a very long time.

Mamm started reading. "Hmm. Seems he's invited

himself to your farm. That's quite rude. I'm a little shocked. He's got no manners at all if he thinks it's okay to invite himself somewhere. It's typical, not unlike the way he thought we wouldn't mind him talking to Cherish away from us. What did he have to say that he couldn't say in front of us.?"

"I said he could come to the farm, *Mamm*. He didn't invite himself."

Ada said, "Yes, Wilma, he's not a rude boy. I told you I'm good friends with his parents and Melvin and Harriet have raised him well. "

"He's not a boy, he's a man," Cherish pointed out.

Ada continued, "He's been taught right from wrong. He's a good young man. You really should trust my judgement more, Wilma. Look how well I matched Mercy and Stephen. Then I was able to match your second oldest daughter as well. I have a gift for this kind of thing."

Cherish sat there in silence, keeping her lips closed. Ada didn't match Honor at all. Honor matched herself and now Ada was taking the credit for it. But wait, did Ada have anything to do with Simon turning up on her doorstep the day after Hope's wedding? "Did you tell Simon about me, Ada?"

CHAPTER 3

*A*da shook her head. "No. I never said two words about you. I thought you met him at the wedding."

Cherish was relieved. Ada said she hadn't match-made them, and Ada would never lie. "I did."

Wilma gulped as she stared at Simon's letter. Her last visit with Mercy played through her mind. Mercy hadn't been getting along that well with Stephen, and Wilma couldn't help wondering if that was a result of the marriage being hasty. If they'd taken longer to get to know each other, Mercy would've probably realized that Stephen got on her nerves most of the time. Still, Stephen was a good person and a good father to their two children. Mercy would have to learn to adjust.

The last thing Wilma wanted was for Cherish or any of her girls to suffer a similar fate. It was so hard to tell the young they didn't have to rush into something when rushing in was all they wanted to do. Mercy had only been eighteen when she married and so too was Honor. There was no need for Cherish to repeat that pattern.

Then and there, Wilma decided she was going to prevent Cherish and Favor, her two youngest daughters, from marrying until they were well into their twenties. "There's only one thing for it."

"What's that, *Mamm?*" Cherish asked.

"I'll have to go to the farm with you next time."

"You will?" Cherish jumped to her feet and ran around the other side of the table to hug her mother.

Wilma put up her hand. "Not so fast. I will, but I never said when."

"Well... when?" Ada asked. "Now that you've said that much, you have to give her a time."

Wilma handed Cherish the letter while she stared up at the ceiling. "We can't go at harvest time. No, that wouldn't do. We'll go in January, in the new year just after Christmas. It's coming up soon, but it's the time of year when we don't have many commitments."

Cherish was delighted to hear that since it was only weeks away. "Okay." Cherish folded her letter and held it tightly in her hand.

"Just remember this." *Mamm* shook a finger at her. "If you rush into marriage, you might spend your lifetime regretting it."

"What's that got to do with going to the farm?" Cherish asked.

Ada busied herself cutting the chocolate cake that was in the center of the table.

Mamm looked down at the letter in Cherish's hand. "I think you know. Just remember this, you are special. Just wait. You'll have your choice of men when you're older. Don't jump on the first train that comes to the station. There's always another train, always a better train. Maybe there's already a train that's been waiting at the station and you haven't noticed it yet. When the time's right, you'll see that train and all will be well."

"Oh, that's confusing." Cherish saw how serious her mother was and did her best to hold in her laughter. "How will I know which train is the right one?"

"You'll just know."

"But what if I don't?" Cherish asked.

"You will."

"But how?"

Wilma threw her hands in the air. "All these questions. You haven't changed since you were three-years-old. 'Why,' 'how,' and 'what for' were your favorite words."

"You're the one who brought up the trains. Now I'm confused."

Wilma explained, "Sometimes it's the ones who are overlooked who make the best husbands. Just because someone is loud and makes their feelings known, doesn't mean that man will make a good husband. That's why you have to wait and make sure you've considered all your options."

Ada looked up from the large slab of chocolate cake she'd served herself. "Samuel was quiet. I had my choice of men, but there was just something about Samuel. One day, we were both helping out at an auction and then he started talking to me. I liked what he said and then we were together every Sunday from there. We got married three months later."

Cherish nodded at Ada's story, pretending she was listening, but she was too excited about going to the farm. Cherish looked at her mother. "I'll make sure I consider the quiet trains as well as the rattling, noisy ones—also the ones that aren't moving to go anywhere. Although, that does sound uninspiring."

"Good."

Ada's brow furrowed. "Wait a minute. Who's catching a train and where is that person going?"

"No one. I just told Cherish I'd take her back to the farm," Wilma said.

"I heard that, but there are no trains that go to the farm."

"I know. I just told Cherish I'll take her to the farm just after Christmas. Weren't you listening?"

"I was thinking about something else, and I was cutting the cake. I can do two things at once but I can't do three!" Ada stared at Wilma.

"We might even see if Favor wants to go with us. It'll be a little getaway for both my girls. Bliss and Debbie can be in charge of the *haus*. I won't tell Favor just yet. I'll make it a surprise."

Cherish hoped Bliss wasn't anywhere close enough to overhear what Wilma just said. It would make her feel ten times worse. Bliss considered Wilma as her mother, but it was clear Wilma didn't quite return that feeling.

"When did you say you were going?" Ada asked.

"In a few weeks. Just after Christmas and into the new year," Wilma repeated.

"That's *wunderbaar*, Cherish. You'll be able to see Simon again."

Mamm turned away, picked up the teakettle and filled it with water while Ada and Cherish talked about Simon.

When they were all sitting, drinking a second pot of tea, Ada broke some very different news. "Just this morning I got some news right from the bishop's wife's mouth."

CHAPTER 4

"What's that?" Wilma stared at Ada. Ada always got interesting information from the bishop's wife.

"John Bontrager's parents are coming to stay with them for a couple of days."

"Staying with the bishop?" *Mamm* asked.

"Correct. They're coming here to see Debbie. Does she know this?"

"No. When are they arriving?" *Mamm* wriggled in her chair.

"They asked to stay with the bishop for two nights. Starting from tomorrow night. They'll want to see Jared."

Mamm nodded. "Of course. That's why they're coming."

Cherish said, "She knew they were coming but they didn't say exactly when. All they said in their letter was they were coming after Hope's wedding."

"And it's after Hope's wedding now." Ada put the teacup up to her lips and took a sip.

SAMANTHA PRICE

"I just hope they don't upset Debbie." *Mamm* looked down at the table.

Cherish bit her lip, worried about how easily Debbie could be pushed around. She had allowed her late husband to push her around and, he had talked her into the secret marriage in the first place. "Of course they will upset her. They want her to live with them and they're very persuasive, and Debbie is fragile at the moment. I'm worried she'll cave."

"Cave?" Ada asked. "What does that mean?"

"Give in to them. She might. She likes to keep everyone happy even if it disadvantages herself."

Ada and Wilma looked at one another. "This isn't good, Wilma. Is Cherish right?"

"I hope not. We don't want to lose her and little Jared." Wilma sighed. "They've only been here for a few months and now I can't imagine them being gone."

"Me either," said Ada. "We've grown so close with her. We'd be losing a good friend. Oh, I don't want to even think about it."

"Cherish, go upstairs and have Debbie come down here."

"Okay." Cherish headed up the stairs. She knew better than to deliver the news Ada had just given her. Ada or *Mamm* would want to tell her themselves. Cherish heard noises coming from the sewing room that had been converted to a nursery. She pushed the door open slightly to see Debbie changing Jared's diaper.

"Hi, Cherish."

"Good morning. Ada is here."

"I know. I saw her out the window. I'm coming down after I change him. Everything okay?"

"Yes." Cherish moved further into the room. "Can I help you with anything?"

"No, but thanks. All done." Debbie lifted Jared up, settled him on one hip, and started walking out the door. Cherish followed them down the stairs.

When Ada saw Jared in Debbie's arms, she immediately got off her chair and stretched her arms out for him. Debbie handed him over.

"Cherish, make some tea for Debbie," *Mamm* said.

"Which tea would you like?" Cherish asked.

"Just some of my rose tea please."

"Rose tea for a rose." Ada smiled as she sat down with the baby. "He's getting so big. Every day I see him, he's bigger."

"Really? I don't notice it except his clothes seem to be getting smaller."

Then Ada and Wilma looked at one another.

"What's going on?" Debbie asked.

Ada spoke. "There's no easy way to say this. I heard from Hannah, the bishop's wife. She told me that John's parents are coming. They've asked to stay there for a couple of nights starting from tomorrow night."

Debbie slumped back in her chair, totally deflated. "I hoped it would be too far for them to come."

Cherish put the teacup and saucer down in front of Debbie and then sat next to her.

"Oh, Cherish. I brought cookies as well as the cake. Would you be a dear and put a few of them on a plate?" Ada asked.

"Sure." Cherish didn't mind doing that. She loved Ada's cookies. Besides, she could eat one or two of the cookies while she was doing it. That way, *Mamm* wouldn't be able to count how many she had. *Mamm* always tried to stop her at three.

Debbie sighed. "I hoped they wouldn't come. You know when people say they'll do something someday, and then they never do it? That's what I was hoping for."

"They want her to move in with them," Cherish said with crumbs flying out of her mouth.

Ada looked up at her. "We know this and don't talk with cookies in your mouth."

"Sorry."

"Be sure to do what *you* want to do, Debbie," Wilma said.

"I want to stay here."

"Don't get bullied into going with them then," Ada told her.

"That's what I'm worried about. I don't want to, but I can't help feeling sorry for them. Now that I've had Jared, it makes me feel how awful it is for them to have lost John."

"They haven't lost him. He's in the Lord's *haus*. They know where he is," Ada said.

Wilma continued, "Life has hardships, but sometimes we can make things harder for ourselves for no good reason. Sometimes in life you have to do what *you* want, especially where there's a child involved. Jared will be happiest where you are happiest."

"Do you think so?" Debbie asked Wilma.

"I do. It makes sense."

Debbie held her head. "I can't help feeling guilty. They live so far away they'll hardly ever get to see him."

"With how they raised John, it's probably a good thing." Cherish placed the plate of cookies into the center of the table and sat down. When she noticed it was quiet, she looked around to see everyone looking at her. "What? It's the truth."

Wilma said, "Debbie doesn't want to hear his name all the time."

Ada added, "They can't be responsible for what their son did, just as Wilma can't be responsible for all the stupid things you girls do."

Cherish kept quiet and reached for another cookie, thinking about what stupid things Ada was talking about. She didn't think about that for long because she was too busy enjoying how the chocolate pieces melted in her mouth and how the cookie part was all buttery and smooth. This batch was well-done on the edges as though Ada had left them in the oven for a little too long. For Cherish, that made them even more tasty.

"I'll just have to get through it and get past it. I know it will be unpleasant for them and for me. I wonder why they didn't write and tell me the date and the day they were coming."

"Maybe they were going to surprise you," Wilma said.

Ada took another sip of tea. "If they're staying at the bishops' tomorrow night, that means they'll be traveling tomorrow and then they'll come here the day after that."

"That makes sense. I'll have to prepare what I'm going to say to them. I'm glad I got some warning. Thanks, Ada."

"Aren't you seeing Peter today?" Ada asked.

"I am. I nearly forgot. I remembered when I woke up, but forgot just now with the news of John's parents."

"Go out and enjoy yourself. We'll look after Jared," Wilma said.

"Thanks, but I'll take him with me this time. Peter said he wants to get to know him."

Cherish swallowed her mouthful of cookie. "That'll be the first time you've gone out together, just the three of you."

"I know."

"And how is Bliss doing?" Ada asked.

"She's in her room, totally depressed about the breakup with Adam," *Mamm* said.

"Totally," Debbie agreed. "I wish there was some way we could make her feel better."

"After your chores, Cherish, why don't you take one of the buggies and get her out of the house?"

"Okay. Where should we go?"

"That's between you and her."

"*Denke, Mamm.* I think she needs to think about something else."

After Wilma told Cherish that three cookies were enough, Cherish walked upstairs smiling about her mother not noticing the cookie she'd eaten before setting the plate on the table.

CHAPTER 5

*C*herish knocked on Bliss's door.

"Come in."

Cherish pushed the door open. Bliss was lying there, looking up at the ceiling.

"I would've come up sooner, but *Mamm* grabbed the letter and read it. Then we found out Debbie's parents are most likely coming here tomorrow."

Bliss sat up. "Was the letter good news?"

Cherish sat down next to her. "Yes." She handed the letter over to let Bliss read it.

"That's great. I'm happy for you." Bliss smiled and handed it back to her. "I'm glad things are going well for one of us."

"Not only that, *Mamm* is taking me to the farm just after Christmas. Well, in early January, she said."

"Truly?"

"Yes, she was the one who said it. She said it just now in front of Ada, so she won't go back on it."

"You'll be able to see Simon much sooner than you thought."

"And I've got some good news for you."

Bliss's face lit up. "About Adam?"

"No, about today. *Mamm* said we could go into town after our chores. Wait, no. She said I could take you somewhere. I just added that bit about town because I thought that's where you'd want to go."

"Really? We get to go out?" Bliss looked happier.

"Yes. Where do you want to go?"

"Anywhere," Bliss said. "You choose. I'm having trouble concentrating. It hurts my head to think."

"Let's get ice-cream."

Bliss laughed. "It's freezing outside. Are you sure you want ice-cream?"

"Maybe not. We'll drive around until we see some nice food. Food that will make you feel better."

"Okay. Thanks, Cherish. I'd really like that."

"I have to do chores first. I think *Mamm's* letting you off chores for the day."

"It's all right. I can't leave everyone else to do everything. I'll come down and help."

"Okay. If you want."

The two girls headed downstairs.

After they spent a couple of hours doing chores, Wilma allowed Cherish and Favor to take Bliss out for the rest of the day. Bliss insisted on driving the horse and buggy, and Favor insisted on sitting next to her so Cherish was relegated to the back seat.

A few minutes into the drive, Favor announced, "I know a great hamburger place."

"That sounds good. I'm so hungry," Cherish said.

"I'm not." Bliss shook her head. "I haven't had any appetite since Adam dumped me."

"As soon as you smell these burgers, you'll be hungry. They're sooo good."

"Okay. I'm willing to give it a try. Where is this burger place?"

"It's right in the center of town."

"Really? Oh no. I don't want to see anyone. I probably should've stayed at home." Bliss rubbed her face with her hands, taking her hands off the reins.

"No. You have to get out and forget about Adam. I find that when I'm unhappy, I feel better if I make myself smile," Favor suggested.

Bliss sighed again. She'd been doing a lot of that lately. "I'll need more than a fake smile to feel better, Favor."

"It's not fake. It is when you start, but pretty soon it becomes a real smile."

From the back seat, Cherish rolled her eyes at Favor. She wasn't helping at all.

Then Favor had an even worse suggestion. "Maybe after our burgers we can visit Krystal."

Cherish leaned over to the front. "No. This outing is for Bliss. We're trying to make her feel better. We're not going to do things that you want."

"The thing is, I don't know what I want anymore, Cherish. Going out was a mistake. I can't be around people. I'm going to turn around."

"No, Bliss. You have to force yourself or you'll end up a cranky and lonely old lady."

25

Bliss said nothing and pretty soon, Cherish noticed Bliss wiping her cheeks.

"Nice one, Cherish." Favor turned around and glared at her.

"I thought I'd be married to Adam next year. Now, I'm alone and I will die alone."

Favor patted Bliss's arm. "That's what we all thought about Florence, but even she found someone."

"Pull over, Bliss. You're in no state to drive." They hadn't gotten into town just yet. Bliss did what Cherish said and then both Bliss and Favor got into the back seat. Cherish moved the buggy forward. "I didn't mean to upset you, Bliss. I just want you to be happy. If you don't marry Adam, you'll marry someone else. If he doesn't know what a wonderful woman you are, he doesn't deserve you. Don't you agree?"

"I guess it's just that he's got standards and I failed to meet them."

"Everyone makes mistakes though," Favor told Bliss. "He's got to see that and when he does, he'll be back."

"Favor's right. Are you telling me he's never made one mistake?"

"He wouldn't have. He's perfect and so honorable, that's why he's so disappointed in me. He needs someone just as good as he is. I failed."

Cherish silently agreed with Bliss about Adam being perfect. As far as she could tell, Adam was perfect in every way, but... Hmm. Maybe that 'perfection' was his flaw? Who was really that perfect? Surely he'd made one mistake, and maybe if she could find out about it, she could point out to him how hypocritical he was being.

A SEASON FOR CHANGE

Talking to him hadn't worked, so she had nothing to lose by trying something different. "Come on, he can't be perfect. Has he made a mistake that you know about?"

"No. He hasn't. He doesn't make mistakes," Bliss said. "Everything he does is carefully thought out, in his business and his relationships."

The rest of the trip was spent in silence.

CHAPTER 6

When they got into town, Favor directed Cherish where to park the buggy. They ended up in a side-street not far from the hamburger destination.

Once they were out of the buggy and walking up the street, Cherish asked, "How do you know about this place, Favor? I've never been here before."

"I've been here a couple of times with Krystal."

They walked in and immediately the smell of the hamburgers hit their nostrils. "See, Bliss? What did I tell you?"

"I'm still not hungry."

"You will be once you taste them. I'll get them. You two sit down. What does everyone want?"

"Nothing. I'll just have an orange juice."

"Boring. I'll order for you. What about you, Cherish?"

"Surprise me. Get me what you're getting."

"Okay. Three burgers with the works and three choco-late shakes."

As Favor walked off to the counter to order, Bliss and Cherish sat down in a booth.

"It's so nice here, don't you think?"

Bliss's gaze lowered to the black and white checkered floor and then went up the pastel colored walls to the old-fashioned stamped metal ceiling. "Yes. It's nice."

"And aren't you glad to be out of the house?" Cherish asked.

"I am."

Cherish was determined to get Bliss to smile before the day was out. No, to laugh. She hadn't done that in ages. "I just want to say this. Adam is great, sure he is, but there are a lot of other great men. He's not the only one who's nice."

Bliss looked down. "He was the only one for me."

Cherish swallowed hard. This wasn't going in the right direction. She thought about what her mother said. "Men are like trains. There will always be another one coming to the station."

Bliss's eyebrows drew together. "What? Stop it, Cherish. How is a man like a train?"

Cherish shrugged. "I don't know. It didn't make much sense to me either. It was something *Mamm* said. She doesn't want me to rush into a relationship. I don't think she wants me to like Simon, or something."

"She just doesn't want you and Favor to marry and leave her alone, but she doesn't have to worry about that because I'll be there forever to keep her company. I'll be living at the apple orchard forever. Until I'm an old lady. I'll die alone under an apple tree, a sad and lonely old wretch."

Favor sat down. "Why are you both looking so weird?"

"Nothing," Cherish said.

"It's coming to the end of the year. Why don't we say what new things we're going to do next year? I'll start. I'm going to have a break from writing to my pen pals. Your turn, Cherish."

"Why are you doing that?" Cherish asked.

"So I'll have time to do other things. Don't ask dumb questions. It's your turn, just say something."

Cherish announced, "I'm going to go back to the farm."

Favor frowned. "It's not something you're going to do. You have to say your intention for the whole year. It's a change in habit or a change of attitude."

"It's too far off. How will I know what I'm going to do?"

"You're so stupid, Cherish. You set an intention so you can follow through."

The waitress brought over their milkshakes.

When she left, Favor turned to Bliss. "What about you?"

"Next year, I'll do my best to stop thinking about Adam."

Favor picked up her milkshake. "I'll say cheers to that."

Bliss picked up her milkshake and they clicked the glasses together.

Cherish guessed that was something Favor picked up from being around Krystal too much. Their mother wouldn't approve. But there was a glimmer of a smile around Bliss's lips, so that was a good thing.

"I want to get better at sewing. Will that do?" Cherish asked.

"Yes. I'll cheers you to that." Favor picked up her milkshake and wanted Cherish to do the same.

"I don't do cheers. The glass might break."

"Suit yourself." Favor took a sip.

"Isn't it great to have a day away from the orchard?" Cherish asked.

"It is. I love it. If only *Dat* would let me work in a place like this." Bliss looked around.

"No. We're destined to only ever work in the orchard. Well, I would be except I've got the farm."

"And, you're also allowed to work at the café one day a week. I don't know why they won't let me." Bliss sat there looking glum.

"It's not *Mamm* not letting you, it's only Levi. Hey, wait. Since you're so upset lately, it's a perfect time to ask your father."

"Ask him if I can start work again at the café?" Bliss sat up straighter.

"Yes. They're looking for workers now too."

"Are they?"

Cherish nodded. "I think so."

Favor interrupted, "You don't seem certain, Cherish. Are they looking for staff or not?"

"I know they were a few weeks ago." Cherish turned her attention back to Bliss. "And anyway, they think you're a great worker."

"Thanks. I'll ask *Dat* tonight. It would really help take my mind off Adam. We're not so busy in the orchard this time of year. I know we've got other chores and we've got the quilt to sew, but it's still nice to get out and see other people. I've missed that."

"I like to see Krystal when I go anywhere. It was so good when she lived with us, don't you think?" Favor asked.

Cherish shook her head. "No, not really."

Favor huffed. "You wouldn't."

At that moment, their burgers arrived.

"What do you think, girls?" Favor stared at the large burgers.

Bliss said, "It looks difficult to eat."

"I like to eat things with a knife and fork," Cherish said.

"Then you both shouldn't have said you'd have a burger." Favor opened her mouth wide and munched into her burger with the works.

Cherish opened her burger and rearranged some items, closed it up again, cut it in half, and then picked up one half of the sandwich and started eating. "Mmm, it is tasty."

"Bliss, come on. Just try a little bit."

"I'll ask for it to go. I might feel hungry later."

"Then at least have some milkshake," Favor said.

Bliss picked up her shake and had a swallow.

"So are you going to marry Simon?" Favor asked Cherish.

"I'd like to get to know him better."

"He seems nice, but you can't get married before me. I'll have to find someone quickly," Favor said.

Since she wasn't eating, Bliss kept her fingers busy by

playing with one of the tiny packets of sugar from the little bowl on the table.

"And how good is it that he lives close to the farm?"

"That is good," Bliss said. "Very convenient."

"You should really try to eat something," Favor said to Bliss. "It's delicious."

"I'll eat it later."

"You better or you'll waste away to nothingness."

"That's the least of my problems."

Favor and Cherish looked at each other. They weren't being very successful in cheering her up.

"What would you like to do when we leave here?" Cherish asked.

"I don't know. All my free time for the last two years was taken up by Adam, so I don't really know what I like to do anymore. Other people have hobbies, but my hobby was Adam."

"What you need is a new hobby."

"I know, but now we all have the quilt to sew. That will keep my mind busy."

"Maybe you should have something else. Something that is yours alone."

Bliss popped the packet of sugar in the bowl with the others as she looked up at Cherish. "I'm not against that idea. What do you suggest?"

"Um." Cherish had no idea so she looked at Favor, hoping she'd say something.

Favor just sat there, eating.

Cherish suggested, "What about basket making? I did some at the farm and I loved it."

"It doesn't interest me. I've always thought I'd like to

draw. I used to do that when I was younger. My mother used to draw and she'd send people post cards that she drew herself. It's like a letter on one side with a picture on the other."

"That sounds like a great idea. What do you need to start off with?" Favor asked. "We could get some things before we go home."

"I'd like that. We'd need some thick drawing paper and some different hardnesses of lead pencils. I'll start off by sketching the orchard. Some of the trees have such interesting formations."

By the time they were ready to go, Bliss seemed more like her old self. The waitress put Bliss's burger in a small box to go, and as the girls were walking out the door, Favor said, "Last one to the buggy has to do the washing up and the drying tonight."

Favor ran off first, followed by Cherish. Normally Bliss wouldn't be bothered to join in, but today she did. She overtook the girls. "You're letting me win," she called over her shoulder.

Then as Bliss turned the corner, she ran smack into something hard. She'd run into a person. She looked up, straight into the eyes of Adam Wengerd, the man who'd broken her heart.

CHAPTER 7

*A*fter Bliss realized she'd run into Adam, she was frozen to the spot.

She didn't know where to look.

He stood there, scowling at the hamburger that had broken out of the box. Ketchup was everywhere, making it look like one of them had suffered a serious injury.

"Are you all right?" Adam's voice didn't sound as annoyed as he looked.

"I think so. Are you?"

He then looked down at his shirt and said nothing.

"I'm so sorry. Your shirt is ruined. I'll wash it for you. I'm sure I can get the stains out."

"No. It's fine. I've got plenty more shirts."

She picked up the flattened box that the burger had come in. She straightened it out so she could put all the mess on top of it.

He stepped back when she tried to get some ketchup and lettuce off his shirt. "It's okay."

She looked down and saw an onion ring clinging to the

middle of her apron. She peeled it off and then knelt down and picked up the burger bun that was on the ground.

He got down on one knee and helped her put all the scraps back into the box. "Let me buy you another..."

"It was a burger, but no thanks. I'm not hungry anyway."

"Are you sure?"

"Quite sure."

Behind them, Cherish and Favor huddled together looking on.

Adam then took the box from her and stood up. "I'll get rid of it." He walked away and put the remains in a nearby trash can. Then instead of coming back to talk to her, he just called out goodbye and walked off as he dusted off his hands.

Bliss looked at Cherish and Favor and they looked back at her. Then Bliss ran to the buggy. Cherish and Favor hurried after her.

When Favor and Cherish reached the horse and buggy, Bliss was in the back seat, crying.

"What did he say?" Favor climbed in next to her.

"Nothing. And then he walked away. Why did I have to come here today? I didn't want to. Everyone forced me."

"Good news. You won the race to the buggy. Cherish and I will do the washing up."

"I don't care," Bliss said. "I just want to go home."

"I'll go back and get you something else to eat," Favor said.

"No! I'm not hungry."

"I'll get you something for later."

"No. Please, Favor, I just want to go home. Right now."

Cherish was in the driver's seat. "I do think you need to try to eat something. Get her a ham and cheese sandwich. I know she likes those," Cherish told Favor.

"Okay." Favor leaped out of the buggy before Bliss could stop her.

"Why are you doing this to me, Cherish? I just want to go home."

"You have to eat. We're worried about you."

"I'm fine. I will be fine when I get home. I wish I'd never left the house."

Cherish didn't know what to do. This whole thing had been a disaster. Where had Adam been going before the collision? And, why had he turned around and walked in the opposite direction afterwards? He was acting so mean and he had to know how kind and soft-hearted Bliss was.

"I'm sorry, Cherish. I know you and Favor are trying to help, but I don't want to be helped."

"There must be something we can do."

"There is. Leave me alone."

Cherish faced the front. Now everything was so much worse. Adam had smiled at Bliss, but he only spoke to her about the hamburger.

"What's taking her so long? Why are people trying to force me to eat?"

"You need to eat, Bliss, that's why."

"I don't have to eat every single day."

"Of course you do. You need three meals every day."

"Or what? I won't die."

Cherish didn't know what to say. She'd never seen

39

Bliss so disagreeable like this, and Bliss was normally someone who enjoyed her food.

A few silent minutes later, Favor was back with the take-out sandwich.

"Now we can find an art supplies shop."

"No. I don't want to do that anymore. I don't want to do anything. Let me drive, Cherish."

"No. You're too upset to drive."

"Are you going to take me home now, Cherish? Because if you don't, I'm getting out of the buggy right now."

Cherish exhaled deeply. "Relax, we're going home." Cherish moved the horse forward.

The drive home was spent in silence.

CHAPTER 8

*W*hen they pulled up at home, Bliss jumped out of the buggy and ran into the house.

"I'll go after her," Favor said.

"No. Just leave her alone for a while."

"I don't take orders from you!" Favor got out of the buggy and headed to the house, leaving Cherish to unhitch the buggy and tend to the horse. It was typical.

When Cherish walked into the house, the first person she saw was Levi. He looked up from the newspaper he was reading. "Bliss just told me she's going into her room and never coming out. What happened today? Wilma said she let you and Favor go out today to cheer her up."

Cherish shook her head. "She's not doing well. She literally bumped into Adam and then he was so short with her. A hamburger got squashed between them and he said a few words, helped her pick up the hamburger and then he left."

He gave a nod. "Favor told me as much. She's up there now trying to comfort her. I'm not sure how to fix this."

Levi folded his paper, leaned forward and placed it on the table beside him.

"Are you thinking of talking to Adam?"

"No. I'm wondering if Bliss should go somewhere. I could send her to a relative for a vacation."

"She wouldn't like that. She'd want to stay here in case Adam changes his mind."

He picked up his large black Bible from underneath the newspaper. "We can pray about it, but if he's not the right man for her, it'll not work out the way she wants—not right now. She'll see later that it's the right thing."

"But couldn't Adam be the right man if we pray that he is?"

Levi stroked his graying beard. "I don't think it works like that. We pray that His will be done. We should go back to having our nightly Bible readings."

"Yes, I think that'll help."

Wilma walked into the room. "Don't be sarcastic, Cherish."

Cherish swung around to face her mother. "I'm not. I think it'll help her. I'm being honest."

"So do I, but I didn't think you would."

Cherish didn't know what to say. Her mother must've been thinking she was a dreadful person.

"That's settled. We'll start our readings again tonight," Levi said.

"Good," Wilma nodded. "I don't know why we ever stopped."

"It was my heart attack. We never—"

"Ah, that's right. That changed our routine a lot."

Cherish slumped into the couch. Levi said he wanted

to do something, but was doing a Bible reading going to help matters? Didn't faith need action as well? The Bible said faith needs works, that was one thing Cherish knew. After what her mother had just said to her, she didn't feel like saying that to Levi.

If Levi wasn't going to act, Cherish knew it was up to her.

She had to find out more about Adam and his past. There was one person in the community who probably knew everything about Adam and that was his good friend and business partner, Andrew Weeks. Now she just had to figure out how to get Andrew to talk with her about Adam.

But her plans would have to wait. Tomorrow, John's parents were coming to see Debbie. Everyone was going to stay home to support her.

"There's one thing that might help, Levi." He kept reading and didn't even look at her.

"What about allowing her to do a day a week at the café? She loved it when she worked there before and then she'd be meeting different people and it would take her mind off Adam."

"That's something to think about." And that was all that Levi said about the matter. Cherish knew not to push him, but at least she'd planted a seed.

CHAPTER 9

*T*he next morning, Levi opened the door to John's parents, Nehemiah and Rebekah Bontrager. They introduced themselves and Levi brought them into the house. Everyone was gathered in the living room. Wilma sent Favor, Cherish and Bliss into the kitchen to make tea and coffee.

Nehemiah moved in front of everyone and sat in Levi's chair. Debbie stared at him and wondered if she should say something. Then she looked at Levi, who appeared slightly disturbed. No one sat in Levi's chair—ever.

Rebekah sat in the smaller chair next to Levi's, which was Wilma's new chair.

Wilma, Levi and Debbie went across and sat down on the couch. What was she supposed to say to her late husband's parents? They had known nothing of the secret marriage and it would've stayed a secret if she hadn't gotten pregnant. Even at John's funeral, before she knew she was pregnant, Debbie felt she should keep the marriage a secret. That was what John had wanted, but she never wanted a stupid secret marriage.

As Debbie sat across from the Bontragers, she wondered why John had been so reluctant to tell them about the marriage. He had to have been embarrassed about being married to her. That, and he knew his parents wanted him to marry Mary Smith. They were her parents-in-law, but without John here and with him having kept their marriage hidden from them, she had no such feelings toward them. None at all.

"Thank you for allowing us to speak with Debbie," Nehemiah said to Levi. "We trust you knew we were coming?"

"We did," Levi replied.

"Could we speak with Debbie alone?" Rebekah asked.

"No," Wilma said. "We'll stay."

The Bontragers looked at each other, then Nehemiah started, "We're here, Debbie, because we are offering for you to come back with us."

"Tell her the other thing, Nehemiah," Rebekah whispered to him.

"We bought you a house, Debbie. It's not far from us, and we thought you'd like your privacy rather than coming to live with us and John's younger brothers."

"You bought me a house?"

"We did," said Rebekah. "We had a talk about it and decided that would be best. We wanted to make sure you'd be comfortable. This is the way for us to show you how serious we are about being close to both you and Jared. After all, you're the only reminders we have of John. And why wouldn't we want our grandson close to us?"

Nehemiah said, "You never have to worry about another thing. It's a five minute walk to our house."

Rebekah started saying, "It's three bedrooms and—"

Nehemiah cut her off. "We don't need to go into all the details now, Rebekah. You'll like it, Debbie. It's a good house."

"I'm... stunned. You bought me a house?" Debbie repeated, trying to let it sink in.

"Yes. We thought you'd like to have your own place rather than live with other people." He gave Levi and Wilma a sidelong glance.

Debbie didn't know what to say. She never thought she'd have a house—ever—unless she married again.

Wilma interrupted, "Debbie is starting her own business."

"Oh, Debbie, you won't need to work if you come back with us." Rebekah shook her head as though having her own business was a dreadful idea.

Nehemiah was quick to agree. "That's right. Your house is waiting and all you need to worry about is raising little Jared. We'll look after everything else for you."

"We're not making her work." Wilma sounded more than a little annoyed.

Levi touched Wilma's arm lightly, and then said, "Debbie has an interest in tea and that's why she's pursuing that line of work."

"Bah, work!" Rebekah swiped a hand through the air. "Work is for men. You're a woman, Debbie. As soon as you come back with us your life will be easy."

Levi cleared his throat. "We told Debbie she's welcome

to stay with us for as long as she likes. She's part of our family."

"That's right, she's our niece," Wilma said.

Nehemiah looked at Wilma. "She's Levi's niece. She's not *your* niece, is she, Wilma? She's only *your* niece because you married Levi. We're Jared's grandparents."

Wilma narrowed her eyes at him, but before she could respond, Rebekah spoke. "We bought the house for you because we knew that's what John would've wanted."

From the kitchen, Favor whispered to Cherish, "Oh, that was mean."

Cherish agreed, "They're manipulating Debbie. I hope she doesn't fall for it. I hope they don't keep talking about John. I wish they'd just get up and leave."

Back in the living room, Debbie put her hand to her head which was now aching. She had been prepared to tell them she wouldn't live with them. She wasn't prepared for them to have bought her a house. This was a real shock. As much as *Onkel* Levi and Aunt Wilma had made her welcome, she'd always feel like a guest in their home. She never saw herself living in her own house with just her and Jared. "There's a lot to consider."

"Consider? What is there to *consider?*" Nehemiah asked, clearly not used to anyone resisting his plans.

"Nothing," Rebekah said. "We've done everything for you. Debbie, your new house is waiting for you and Jared. Your parents are also looking forward to you living near them. They knew we bought you a house but we wanted to be the ones to surprise you with the news. They didn't let anything slip, did they?"

Debbie shook her head.

Cherish and Favor looked at each other. "She's not going to go with them, is she?"

Favor shrugged her shoulders. "I don't know. They've bought her a house. I'd go with them. Maybe they'll adopt me. I wouldn't have to work or do anything. They're going to provide for her forever, it seems."

"I know. I heard." Cherish bit her lip and kept listening. Without Debbie, the house would be way too quiet. "Surely she'll choose us. This is so unfair. Why did they have to come here?"

"Shush. I'm listening."

"Move over so I can see what's going on."

"I can't. I'm right against the wall. You move over. You're squashing me."

Bliss sat at the kitchen table. "You two shouldn't be listening."

"How else will we hear what they're saying?" Cherish stepped to the side and now she was in the middle of the doorway. Wilma turned her head and saw Cherish and frowned at her. Cherish moved back so she'd be out of sight.

Nehemiah said, "We're staying in the area for a couple of days, Debbie. That should give you enough time to pack and get your things together."

Rebekah said, "We'll leave early on Friday morning."

"I'll still want to do my tea."

Wilma stared at Debbie. "You're not seriously considering it, are you?" she blurted.

Back in the kitchen, Bliss gasped at what Wilma had said in front of the Bontragers. Cherish and Favor were shocked, too.

CHAPTER 10

*J*ohn's mother stared at Wilma. "She's not just considering it, she's coming back with us. I'm sorry, Wilma. I know you probably got used to her being here, but I hope you didn't think it was going to be permanent. After all, Jared has two sets of grandparents in Willow Valley."

"Are you leaving us, Debbie?" Levi asked.

"No. I mean, I just want to do my tea." Debbie looked down at her hands in her lap.

"You can make your tea here. Thank you for your kind offer, Rebekah and Nehemiah, but Debbie has already said she'd be staying here with us," Levi told the Bontragers.

"But, we bought her a house," Rebekah said. "It's just sitting there empty waiting for her."

"It's okay," Nehemiah told his wife. "Debbie didn't know about this. It's a big change. She'll just have to get used to the idea. Just like we had to get used to the idea that John is no longer with us."

Debbie jumped to her feet. "Excuse me. I think I hear Jared."

Rebekah brightened up. "Oh good. Bring him down so we can meet him. We've been dying to see him."

Without a word, Debbie hurried up the stairs.

Favor left the kitchen and followed her, leaving Cherish in the kitchen with Bliss.

Without knocking, Favor burst into Debbie's room. Debbie was just sitting on the bed and Jared was nowhere to be seen. "You can't go with them, you just can't."

Debbie looked up at her. Favor rushed to her side when she saw tears streaming down Debbie's cheeks. "Don't cry, Debbie. It's going to be okay."

Debbie shook her head and then gasped for air. "I... I'm confused."

"About what?"

"I want to stay here but I feel so bad for them. They lost John, their oldest son, and they bought me a house."

"I know I heard that from the kitchen."

"If I say no, then that would be like throwing it in their faces. It would've cost them a lot."

"You said they're rich."

"They are."

"Did you ever think that they did that just to make sure you went back with them?"

Debbie sniffed. "Do you think so?"

Favor nodded. "Well, John had a certain way about him. He wasn't exactly straightforward with…"

"You mean he wasn't totally honest?"

"That's right, and, from what you said, he was scared

of his parents. That's why he didn't tell them about your marriage."

"What are you saying, Favor?"

"You've got to stand up to them. Don't go along with them like you said everyone else does. Be strong or you'll end up being just like your parents."

"Nehemiah and Rebekah are Jared's grandparents. What do you expect me to do?"

Favor bolted to her feet. "You disappoint me. You said you wouldn't go with them. I don't care that they bought you a house or whatever else they say they're going to do." Favor planted her hands on her hips. "How do you know they won't let you stay in that house for a year and then sell it out from underneath you? Then where will you go?"

"I'd have to move in with them or my parents."

"Exactly."

"I see what you mean."

"They didn't even say they were going to put the house in your name, did they? No, because they've already bought it. So if the house isn't in your name, is it really your house when you don't have a say with what happens to it in the future? They could sell it from underneath you whenever they wanted. It could be their way of controlling you and Jared for years to come."

Debbie's mouth fell open. "Favor, you're so smart. Did you just think of all this now?"

"Yes. I'm just putting two and two together and coming up with 22."

Debbie frowned. "You mean four."

53

"No. Twenty two because you'd expect the answer to be four, but not when you can't trust the people."

"Even if they give me the house as my own, I still don't want to go there."

"Don't do it then."

"I want to stay here with all of you."

"Good. Then go down and tell them that."

Debbie put her hand over her forehead and massaged her temples. "It's so hard. They must feel so bad about what happened with John. Do you think *Onkel* Levi will tell them for me?"

"*Nee*. They wouldn't believe it. It's got to come from you. Of course they'll be upset, but someone's going to be upset and I don't want it to be us."

The bedroom door opened and Cherish slipped into the room. "What's going on?"

"I told you to stay in the kitchen," Favor said.

"I don't take orders from you." Cherish sat on the other side of Debbie. "Tell them you're staying here."

"She doesn't want to hurt their feelings, but I told her it's the only way. They have to hear it."

"What do you want to do, Debbie?" Cherish asked. "Stay with us or go with them?"

"I was just telling Favor I want to be here, but after all John's parents have been through, I know it'll upset them." Debbie swallowed hard. "I told them I heard Jared, but he's still asleep. I just needed to get away from them and think for a while. I lied to them just now."

Cherish said, "*Gott* will forgive you. You're under so much pressure. Just tell them what you honestly want.

54

They wouldn't want you to move there if they knew you want to stay here."

"Maybe they're not thinking of Debbie," Favor said.

"They are thinking of me, they bought me a house."

Favor shrugged her shoulders. "*Jah,* but like I said, is it really yours? And for how long?"

Cherish stared at Favor. "I never thought of that." Favor was a lot smarter than she seemed.

"I guess there's no other way around it. I'll have to tell them."

Favor put her arm around Debbie. "What's the worst thing that can happen if you tell them you're staying put?"

"They'll be upset."

"That's right, so take Jared down with you and they'll be so pleased to see him that they'll get over it."

Debbie bit her lip. "Do you think so?"

"Of course."

At that moment, they heard Jared making noises from his bedroom next door.

"He's awake. I'll have to feed him and then I'll bring him down. Can you tell them I'll be down soon?"

"Okay," Favor said. Then she and Cherish left the room and started walking downstairs.

Cherish whispered to her, "How did you think of that about the house just now?"

"Because John couldn't be trusted. Where did he learn that?"

Cherish opened her mouth in shock. "His parents?" Favor didn't answer except to quirk an eyebrow at her sister, because they were now at the bottom of the stairs.

Everyone looked at them and Favor said, "She'll be down soon."

Cherish and Favor rejoined Bliss in the kitchen. *Mamm* followed them in and asked them what was happening with the tea and coffee they were supposed to be making.

"Are they staying that long?" Cherish asked. "We were waiting to see if they might leave right away."

"Of course they are staying for a good while. They need to see their grandson. Why? What did Debbie say? Is she thinking of leaving us?" *Mamm* set her beady, brown eyes on Favor and then Cherish.

Favor told her, "She says no, but she's also feeling sorry for them."

Mamm shook her head. "They're doing everything they can to make her go with them. How can we keep her? We can't buy her a house. Is that what we need to do?"

"She doesn't want that, *Mamm*. She just wants to stay with us."

"I hope that's enough for her. Wanting to stay with us will have to be stronger than her feeling sorry for them," Bliss said.

"I better get back to them. Levi isn't much of a talker."

Meanwhile, Debbie was upstairs feeding Jared, trying to find the right words to tell the Bontragers she wouldn't be leaving with them. Neither would she be moving into that house they'd bought for her. Pangs of guilt gnawed at her stomach. It would be one of the hardest conversations she'd ever have.

They'd bought her a house! That was a huge thing to do.

How ungrateful would she sound to turn her back on

that? Favor's words echoed through her mind and that led her to wonder, what if it was just some carrot they were dangling?

Then her mind drifted back to before she and John got married. John's parents never saw her as a suitable match for him. Not only that, they wanted him to marry Mary Smith. They never wanted her as a daughter-in-law. That was clear because they never showed her family much respect at all. Her father was just someone who worked for them.

But then again, if she moved to Willow Valley, Jared would grow up near both sets of grandparents.

If she stayed at the Baker Apple Orchard, her son would grow up with Joy's child and Christina's twins, and soon Hope would have children too. There would be loads of children for him to play with, and many adults who loved him. Wilma and Levi would be substitute grandparents along with Ada and Samuel.

Her mind was made up. She'd be strong, follow her heart. People would be disappointed and there might even be tears.

CHAPTER 11

Twenty minutes later, Debbie came downstairs with Jared. She allowed his grandparents to hold him. Jared vomited a little on Rebekah's shoulder, but Rebekah didn't mind. She laughed about it while Wilma and Debbie raced to the kitchen to get something to clean it off.

After a while, Jared started crying so Debbie took him from Rebekah and sat back down. Once the baby was back in his mother's arms, he settled.

After a quick and silent prayer, Debbie began, "I want to thank you both for coming here. It was nice of you to want me to come back with you, but I've decided to stay here."

Rebekah looked at her husband, but he just stared at Debbie and ignored his wife. "Debbie, I can't believe that's best. We have everything there that you could ever need. We have a house there that we bought just for you. Why don't you come back with us for a visit? You can see it and the type of life you could have there."

"Thank you, but I'd rather stay here. I don't like traveling and it would be too difficult with the baby."

Rebekah started crying, and Debbie sat there, not knowing what to do.

Nehemiah patted Rebekah's shoulder, and then looked up and said, "She's upset. We've lost John, and now… it looks like you're denying us our grandchild."

"She's not doing that at all. You're welcome to see Jared anytime you'd like, and see Debbie too," Wilma said.

Rebekah took out a handkerchief and dried her eyes. "We have another idea. Why don't you give the child to us to raise, Debbie? We—"

"She won't be doing that," Levi said firmly.

Debbie held Jared a little bit tighter. No one was taking her child from her.

Wilma stared up at her husband. He normally was so quiet and softly spoken.

Nehemiah grunted. "Levi, with all respect, I think Debbie should be the one making that decision."

Everyone then looked at Debbie.

Debbie looked down at her baby and muttered, "Oh, I don't like to upset anyone."

"Just say what you want," Wilma said. "You must think of what you believe is right for yourself and Jared."

"You didn't let me finish, Levi," Rebekah said. "Can everyone let me say what I have come to say? We came here with two ideas, Debbie. We have bought a house for you and Jared, but then on our way here, we thought about some different ideas. We could raise Jared and then you'd be free to have the life you choose. Everyone would respect that you've put your child first. We can offer the child so much more."

While Rebekah was drawing a breath, Nehemiah jumped in. "You're young enough to marry again and have more babies. If we take Jared off your hands, we'd be setting you free."

Rebekah continued, "Or if you don't like that idea, we'd love for you to leave with us tomorrow and we'll go back to Willow Valley and we'll help you get settled back in."

Debbie took a deep breath. "I'm staying here with Jared. I don't need or want to be *set free* from the child who is a gift from *Gott* to me. That's what I want and I believe that would be best for Jared too."

The Bontragers looked at each other, then Nehemiah said, "I don't think you've thought this through properly, Debbie."

"You've heard her answer, Nehemiah," Levi said. "She's staying here with family."

Nehemiah frowned and then faced Debbie. "Just take a while to think about it, Debbie. Don't let anyone influence you."

"I won't and I haven't. I appreciate you coming here, I do, but my mind's made up."

Rebekah opened her mouth in shock. "You're not leaving with us?"

Debbie shook her head.

"But we bought you a house," Rebekah whimpered.

"I'm sorry, but I wish you would've talked to me before you did that."

"It's done now." Nehemiah leaned over and once again

he patted his wife on her shoulder, then he said to Debbie. "We were fully confident that you'd have the common sense to do the right thing. It seems common sense is not so common anymore. We're offering you everything we can."

"Thank you. I do appreciate it, but staying here is the right thing for me and for Jared."

"We should go now, Rebekah. I'm sure we've given Debbie a lot to think about. We'll be back tomorrow. Just think it over, Debbie. Will you at least agree to think about it some more?"

Debbie wanted to tell them no, and that there was nothing to think about. She couldn't say that, because she felt so sorry for Rebekah what with the way she was looking at Jared. "Okay. I'll do that, but I'm sure my decision will remain the same."

"Thank you," Nehemiah said.

When Rebekah moved to stand up, Levi and Wilma stood too.

Nehemiah turned to face Debbie. "One thing I've been meaning to tell you."

"What's that?"

"We have a few Jareds in the family. Going way back in the family tree."

"I didn't know that. That's a nice coincidence."

"My father's brother was a Jared. Sadly, he died some years ago. Now we have another Jared Bontrager in the family."

Debbie's breath caught in her throat. She swallowed hard looking at both of Jared's grandparents. "Didn't my mother and father tell you?"

Nehemiah stared at her. "Tell us what?"

"Jared's last name is Bruner, same as mine. His name is Jared Bruner."

"No, I mean, you and John were married so the baby takes his name," Rebekah said angrily. "And, so should you."

Debbie shook her head. "I know, but it doesn't have to be like that."

Nehemiah narrowed his eyes at her and then shot Levi an unkind look while Rebekah grabbed hold of his arm as though she was going to faint. "What nonsense is this?" he asked. "Children always take the name of their father. It's tradition."

Debbie regretted telling them face-to-face. They would've found out eventually and then wondered why they were never told. "It was my decision, and mine alone, to change that tradition for myself and for Jared. After all, the marriage was hardly traditional."

"Do you mean to shut us out of your life?" Nehemiah asked.

"Not at all. I think it's important that Jared know about his father's side of the family. The name is something I've done for my own personal reasons."

Nehemiah looked down at his wife. "I think we've stayed too long, Rebekah. It's time to leave." Then he said to Levi, "We'll be back late tomorrow afternoon."

After they said a frosty goodbye, Levi walked them to the door.

Then everyone sat back down. When Debbie heard the hoofbeats of the horse and buggy they'd borrowed from

63

the bishop, she was able to relax a little. They were gone, at least for now.

"How are you feeling, Debbie?" Wilma asked as the girls came out from the kitchen to join them.

"I feel pretty awful. They bought a house for me without even asking me."

"They didn't ask you because they knew you would've said no," Favor said.

"Now they're coming back tomorrow. I feel so sad for them. I know they want to be a part of Jared's life and I can't blame them for that."

"It's not about them, Debbie. It's what's best for you. You're the one raising the child," Wilma said. "And I don't like that they offered to take him away from you and raise him. You're quite capable of doing that yourself."

Debbie slowly nodded, pleased that everyone wanted her there. "I felt so bad for telling them about the last name. I thought my parents would've told them that for sure."

"Well, they know now. There was no easy way of telling them and it's only natural they'd be upset about it," Bliss said.

Cherish laughed. "I loved the way you said the marriage wasn't traditional so you're changing the tradition with the name."

Mamm scowled at her. "Don't take humor in someone else's pain."

"I wasn't. I didn't mean to do that anyway." Cherish bit her lip. She should've just kept quiet.

"They'll get over it in time," Levi said.

"Will they?" Favor asked. "A name is a big thing. It'll be something they'll always think about."

"You're not helping," said Levi.

"It's okay. Don't be mad at anyone. The name's done. It's official and I wouldn't want to change it anyway."

"Let's do something enjoyable with what's left of the day," Wilma said as she took the baby from Debbie.

"I like the sound of that. What should we do?" Bliss asked.

"We can start working on the quilt." Wilma rocked Jared to and fro.

Debbie nodded. "Good idea. That's just what I need to keep my mind off everything."

"Cherish and Favor, you can clear the kitchen table so we can cut the fabric."

Levi stood up. "I'll be out with the horses if anyone needs me."

"Thanks for being here when they came, *Onkel* Levi. It helped."

"We want you here, Debbie. Since that's what you want too, we'll all do everything to have you stay."

Everyone agreed.

CHAPTER 12

The next day, everyone in the Baker/Bruner household, except Levi, was working on the quilt when they heard noises coming from outside. Looking out the window, Bliss yelped, "It's a wagon. Oh no, it's Adam."

Cherish raced to the window and nudged her out of the way. "It's Adam and Andrew. That means they have my aviary ready."

"You didn't tell me he was bringing it today," Wilma whined. "Where will we put it?"

"It can go outside somewhere but not until the warmer weather."

"Why? Birds live outside in the winter."

"Not these birds. They're not used to it."

"They can get used to it."

Bliss recoiled in horror. "I can't let Adam see me. This is awful."

"You can't hide away from him," *Mamm* said. "He'll always be in this community."

"Unless he moves," Favor commented.

"It's not likely with his business doing so well," Bliss added. "I'll be in my room. He's only come to bring the birdcage. He hasn't come to see me."

"Don't be silly, go out and say hello. Go with Cherish," *Mamm* told Bliss.

"No, *Mamm!* The last time we spoke, it didn't go so good. I'll be up in my room." Bliss walked out of the kitchen.

Mamm then stared at Cherish. "Well, go on then. Show him where you want the cage. No good trying to talk to you about where it will go. You've always got your mind made up and you won't listen to sense."

"It's an aviary. I'll have him put it in the barn for now," Cherish said.

"Please yourself. Are you paying for this or do we have to?"

"I'm paying for it."

"That's one blessing."

Cherish walked outside. As soon as she saw Adam, she thought he looked just as uncomfortable as Bliss had looked just now. "You've finished it already?"

He smiled. "I did. Andrew has come along to help me install it."

She looked over at Andrew Weeks, and said hello. Then she wondered how she could get him alone to ask him questions about Adam. "It'll have to go in the barn for now."

"Really?"

"Yes."

"I guess there's no point in us assembling it then. It'll take up less room if we leave it in pieces."

"Great idea. Then you can come back when I'm ready for it? Will that be okay? I wouldn't know how to do it and I'd get it wrong."

"Sure. I was just going to suggest that."

Cherish looked at Andrew. He was much quieter than normal. It was clear he knew what was going on between Adam and Bliss. Probably everyone in the community knew about it by now. "I'll get the money. It's in the house."

"Okay. Shall we just put it anywhere in the barn?"

"Just at the side where it'll be out of the way." Cherish left them and went into the house. When she was up in her bedroom, counting out the money, Bliss walked in. "What did he say?"

"Not much at all. Andrew's with him and they're just putting it in the barn for now."

"Did he say anything about me?"

"No. Don't be upset. He's only here to deliver the aviary, and he wouldn't ask about you in front of Andrew."

Bliss put her hand to her head. "Oh, I hope *Mamm* doesn't invite them in for something to eat."

"Don't worry, I'll tell her not to."

"Thanks."

Cherish finished counting out the money and then left the room with a fistful of notes. Before she walked out of the house, she told her mother to stay put and not to come out of the house. Wilma agreed without asking questions—for once.

By the time Cherish got back outside, the two men had already left the unassembled aviary in the barn and were climbing back into the wagon. "Here's the money," Cherish said when she reached Adam.

"Thank you."

"It's all there. Count it if you want."

"I trust you."

Cherish smiled. "I hope so."

"Say hello to everyone. We can't stay. We've got another delivery to make."

Cherish was still figuring out how to get Andrew on his own to find out more about Adam. Today wasn't going to be the day. "Sure. Well, I guess we'll see you on Sunday. Thanks for making it for me. I can't wait for the birds to be able to use it. I'm sure they'll love it."

"I hope so. Bye, Cherish."

Andrew nodded goodbye, and then Adam wasted no time in turning the wagon around and heading back down the driveway.

When Cherish looked up at the house, she saw everyone appeared in the doorway. They just stood there, looking out. Even Debbie was there with Jared in her arms. They were all waiting to hear what Adam had said.

It was a weird moment. For an instant, Cherish just stood there. This moment would never have happened if she hadn't found those letters in Bliss's room. If she'd known things would be so awful, she would've left things well and truly alone.

Cherish swallowed hard and walked toward her family, wishing she had something better to tell them. She stepped up onto the porch with her footsteps echoing through the air, breaking the silence. "They said they couldn't stay."

Mamm frowned. "You asked me not to come out. Did you invite them in at least?"

"No. When they said they couldn't stay, there was no point inviting them in."

Bliss asked, "Who said they couldn't stay? Was it Andrew or Adam?"

"Adam. He said they had another delivery to make."

"That's reasonable. I'm guessing they're busy. What else did he say?" Debbie asked.

"Just stuff about the aviary, and then he said to say hello to everyone."

Favor gasped. "Oh, Bliss, do you think that was his way of saying hello to you?"

"I don't know. Do you think so?"

Favor looked at Cherish. "What do you think? You were there."

"I don't know." She didn't want to get Bliss's hope's up. "Maybe he was being polite. He didn't say anything about Bliss. Sorry, Bliss."

"Don't be sorry. I don't want you or anyone to lie to me. He hates me now and it might stay that way forever. I could see that when he looked into my eyes."

Mamm clicked her tongue. "He doesn't hate you, Bliss. You shouldn't even think that. He's just a bit upset. You two got along so well. It can't be over. He'll come around given enough time."

"How much time?"

"I don't know. Everyone is different." They all turned and looked when a horse and buggy approached the house. "It's Ada and Samuel. They're staying for the evening meal. They're bringing Levi back," *Mamm* said.

"Where has Levi been?" Favor asked.

"He was giving a friend a helping hand."

Bliss said, "Normally, Adam would've come back to eat with us. Now he's not here. Hope and Fairfax are away too and it'll be just us." Bliss's eyes filled with tears and then she moved into the kitchen.

Everyone looked at each other helplessly as Bliss walked away. No one knew what to do to make her feel better.

Cherish whispered, "I couldn't say he said something he didn't say. He might never want to even be friends with her. He's so upset."

"Just don't tell her that," *Mamm* said.

"I didn't, and I won't."

Mamm sighed. "Maybe Ada can make her feel better."

"Ada?" Favor and Cherish chorused.

"Yes. On the quiet, I'll tell her that Bliss is upset. All of you go inside and start peeling the vegetables. I'll talk to Ada."

While *Mamm* went to talk with Ada, the girls all moved into the kitchen. Cherish looked back at Samuel's buggy and saw Matthew getting out. He'd been working part time at Mark's saddlery store and they hadn't seen much of him. Everything was livelier and a little more fun when Matthew was about.

CHAPTER 13

*A*t dinner that night, everyone knew about what had happened with Bliss and Adam. Wilma had told them all not to mention Adam's name.

"So what happened with your tea tasting, Debbie? Weren't you going to try it out on suspects?" Matthew asked.

Cherish giggled. "You mean prospects."

He grinned. "Depends how good the tea is."

Before Debbie could answer, Cherish spoke for her. "We were all set to try the tea out and get opinions. It's called a focus group, isn't it, Debbie?"

"That's right. We were going to do it and then Jared had a slight cold. He's over it now. Cherish is helping me with it. Who else wants to help me?" Debbie asked.

"We all will," Bliss said. "When do you want to do it?"

"Wilma and I will look after Jared. You just name the day," Ada said.

"How about the day after tomorrow? The Bontragers

would've left by then. I'll have a day to prepare everything."

"That'll work for me," Cherish said. "I work at the café on Friday this week."

"Any day's okay with me," Favor said.

"Thanks, everyone. I really want to start this and see how far I can go with it." Debbie looked at each one of them.

"You can go as far as you want," Samuel said. "There's no stopping people who are excited about what they're doing. Your excitement transfers to others and pretty soon, you reach your goals."

Ada frowned at Samuel and didn't say anything. Samuel saw Ada looking at him and went back to eating.

"I'm so excited. I just hope the people like my tea."

"Of course they will," Wilma said. "Have faith. The only problem they'll have is choosing what flavor they like best."

Debbie was happy with Wilma's comment and hoped that everyone liked her tea as much as her family did.

When dinner was over, Cherish pulled Matthew aside and whispered to him in the corner of the living room. "Matthew, I have a plan to get Adam and Bliss back together."

He frowned. "Since you're telling me, I'm guessing it involves me."

"It could."

"What is it?"

"I need to know if Adam's ever made a mistake."

"What for?"

Cherish took an exasperated deep breath. "You've got to follow me with this. I'm trying to get Adam and Bliss back together. They're made for each other. He's not forgiving her for writing back to John, so I thought if I can find a mistake of his, I can go to him with it. I can make him see that he should forgive Bliss because everyone makes mistakes."

He pushed his hat back on his head slightly. "That's a crazy idea."

"It's not. Well, it might be, but I can't think of anything else. Maybe you could talk to Andrew Weeks and he might tell you something about Adam."

"I doubt it. Men don't gossip like women do."

Cherish hit his arm. "Don't be rude. It's not gossiping."

"Sounds like it to me."

"Will you help or not?"

"I'm willing if you've got a different idea, one that might work."

"I can't think of anything else. It took me long enough to think of this plan. I thought it was a good one."

Matthew shook his head. "It's not. If a man says it's over, that usually means it's over. The trust has been broken and that's a pretty big thing."

"I know, but you don't know Bliss like I do. She's so trustworthy."

"Why did she write to John then?"

Cherish didn't like the question. "It was a lapse in good judgement."

"And how many letters did she write? I heard it was a

few so it's not just one mistake. It's the same mistake repeated all while she was dating Adam. I wouldn't like it."

"Well no one's dating you so you don't have to worry about it."

Matthew chuckled. "No one's dating me yet, but our time will come."

Cherish recoiled from his comment. "Our time? Separately maybe, but not together."

"If you say so."

"I do."

Matthew wasn't offended. "Let me think about it for a while. I'll come up with something better than your idea."

"Thanks. I can't keep seeing her so upset. It's awful feeling so helpless."

"Leave it with me."

Cherish didn't like things being out of her control. "Okay, but don't take too long. It needs to be done quickly."

Ada looked up at them. "What are you two whispering about?"

Matthew left Cherish and headed over to the couch. "Nothing."

"It can't be nothing," Ada said. "It must be something. Care to share? You must know it's rude to whisper in a room full of people."

Cherish said, "I was just trying to get Matthew to help me with something."

Mamm laughed. "It'd be the dishes."

"How did you guess?" Matthew asked.

Cherish went into the kitchen. Favor had already

started the dishes and it was her turn to dry. Cherish picked up a tea towel.

Favor looked over at her. "It sure has been depressing around here lately. I wish Krystal still lived here, that would brighten things up."

Cherish scowled. She couldn't think of anything worse. "I agree about it being awful around here with John's parents visiting. That's got to make Bliss feel worse as well."

"Yeah." Favor plunged a stack of dishes beneath the soapy water. "Our house is like this and it's all because of John. We never even met John but look how he's affecting all of our lives."

Cherish was quiet for a while as she thought about what Favor said. She was right. How could a complete stranger affect the lives of so many of them? "A secret marriage, and before that secret letters. That John guy sure had a lot happening. I wonder if there's more secrets that we haven't found out about yet."

Favor snorted. "I hope not."

CHAPTER 14

*L*ate in the afternoon the next day, John's parents returned. Debbie was nervous, but she was ready. Wilma told the girls to stay in the kitchen and Levi opened the door for the Bontragers. He then led them through to the living room where Debbie and Wilma waited.

They sat down, once again taking Wilma and Levi's chairs. Wilma sat on the couch with Debbie and baby Jared. Levi sat on the other side of them.

Nehemiah broke the awkward silence. "When we came here yesterday, Debbie, we thought you'd be delighted about the house and you'd be coming home with us. We didn't expect we'd be waiting for a decision from you. We thought you'd be only too happy with our generous offer. We've left you alone for a day to think it through."

"What have you decided to do, Debbie?" Rebekah asked.

Debbie took a deep breath. "I'm going to stay here."

Rebekah and Nehemiah stared at each other. Then Rebekah asked, "For how long?"

"They said I can stay here forever if I want."

Nehemiah said, "I don't know what to say."

Debbie lowered her head. "I'm sorry to upset you."

"We thought we'd be taking John's baby home with us," Rebekah whined.

Debbie said, "I'm not keeping him from you. You can see him whenever you want."

Nehemiah moved to the edge of the chair. "It's not easy for us to come here. I have a business to run. It would've been more convenient for us if you'd come with us so we could all be one big happy family."

"We'll try to visit," Debbie said in a small voice.

"Try?" Nehemiah asked.

"That's the best I can do. I have a life here now."

"What life do you have here, Debbie? How can you say you have a life here when you've only been here for a few months?" Rebekah fixed her gaze upon Debbie.

"Exactly," Nehemiah agreed. "You haven't been here long enough to have a life."

Debbie wanted to ask them why they thought she wasn't good enough for John, and why they wanted John to marry Mary. It didn't matter now, she reminded herself. "I feel at home here and this is the only place Jared knows."

"He's too young to even know where he is. Is someone trying to keep you away from us?"

Debbie tilted her head, wondering what he was getting at. "No, not at all."

"That's what it sounds like to us." Rebekah leaned forward and whispered, "Do they have some kind of hold over you? It's all right, you can tell us."

Wilma's mouth fell open. "I hope you're not talking about us."

"We asked yesterday to speak in private and you refused us," Nehemiah said. "If today's rules are different we'd gladly talk to Debbie alone. Otherwise, we must speak freely."

"No one's keeping me here," Debbie said. "They've always been good to me from the start and I get along with every one of them. They've all been good."

"And why wouldn't they be good?"

"I don't know. You just said, do they have a hold over me. It sounds like you think they're forcing me to stay or something."

"We can't think of any other reason you wouldn't come with us. We even bought you a very nice house. We thought you'd be delighted." Rebekah pulled out a white handkerchief and dabbed at her tears.

"I'm very grateful—"

"It's there waiting for you. Your very own house," Rebekah said.

"How else would you ever get a house, unless you marry a widower like your parents are suggesting. Did they mention that to you?" Nehemiah asked.

"Yes. They gave me all their suggestions and that was one of them. I won't be making a marriage of convenience." Debbie shook her head.

"And you don't have to. You see? We think alike. We'll

81

be your family." Rebekah lowered her handkerchief and sniffed a couple of times.

"She is already our family, Rebekah."

"Yes, that's what I meant."

Debbie didn't know what to say. She'd already told them she wasn't going with them and they just wouldn't stop. "I do appreciate you buying the house, but it might've been better to talk to me about it first."

"Then it wouldn't have been a surprise. John loved surprises and being his wife, we thought you would've too. You have to have something in common or he wouldn't have chosen you."

"That's right. Chosen you above the other women who would've liked for him to choose them," Rebekah spat out.

Debbie shook her head. "We must've had other things in common because I don't like surprises. I like to have things planned out and I have planned for my life to be here."

"So you've met another man, have you?" Rebekah fastened her beady eyes upon her.

Debbie nearly choked. "I've met someone I get along with, but we're very far away from anything becoming serious."

A single tear trickled down Rebekah's cheek. "I knew it. Didn't I say that was the reason, Nehemiah? Have you forgotten John so easily?"

"No. I'll never be able to forget him and the secret marriage we had." Now Debbie was starting to get upset. "I didn't want it to be a secret. Maybe he wanted to surprise everyone with it since he liked surprises so much. Seems he liked secrets too as well as surprises."

"That wasn't necessary, Debbie." Nehemiah put his arm around his wife as she sobbed. "We should go. Debbie has made up her mind."

Through her tears Rebekah asked, "Can we see the baby again, Debbie?"

"Of course you can, but he's asleep." She didn't want them to come into his room. "I'll bring him down."

They saw Jared, who remained asleep while they were saying goodbye to him, before they finally left.

"How are you feeling, Debbie?" Wilma asked.

"Pretty drained." She looked down at her sleeping baby. "I didn't want them in his room. I'm not sure why."

"I'll take him upstairs for you," Favor said.

Debbie handed him over to Favor, and he stayed sleeping.

Levi sat down after having walked the Bontragers to the door. "I thought I should keep out of things today. I didn't want to inflame the situation by having my say."

"That was best," Wilma told him.

"What did they say?" Bliss sat next to Debbie.

"Weren't you listening?"

"We heard most of it."

"They made me feel so bad."

"They meant to," Bliss told her. "Don't be concerned about them. I mean it's sad for them, but you have to do what you want to do."

"There is no easy answer in this situation. You did what you had to do. You told them what you wanted and what you thought was best for Jared," Levi told Debbie.

Wilma agreed with him. "And that's all you can do, Debbie."

Debbie nodded and she was pleased she wouldn't have to see John's parents for a very long time. It would take her a while to get over their visit.

CHAPTER 15

*T*hat night, Cherish went up to bed thinking she would drop right off to sleep, but she couldn't. She tossed and turned. After a while, she got up and wrote a letter to Malachi. When she finished that, she wrote a letter to Fenella, her best friend that she met at Miriam and Earl's wedding.

Then, she sneaked into Favor's room and retrieved the women's magazine Favor had hidden under her bed and took it back to bed to read. It was mostly advertisements, so Cherish was soon bored with that.

When she heard talking coming from downstairs, she crept up the hallway. It was *Mamm* and Levi and they were by themselves in the living room.

Cherish lowered herself onto her tummy and moved to the head of the stairs so she could see them and hear them better.

"What did you think about the Bontragers, Levi?" Wilma asked.

"I was upset for them about Jared not carrying on the Bontrager name."

"But you were very happy about it when Debbie told you."

"Of course I was because he is a Bruner now."

"I see." *Mamm* went back to her sewing.

"Names mean a lot." Levi continued reading his Bible.

"I'm finding that out. Ada can talk about nothing else —insisting babies have middle names and such."

"I don't think middle names are as important as she does. Last names are important to a man. Jared is the first grandchild and the first male, and he won't be a Bontrager. Naturally, they're upset by that."

"Oh. I see what you mean. I thought they were getting a bit angry there for a moment. I liked the way you said your piece to them yesterday."

"I didn't come across too strong, did I?" Levi asked.

"No, just perfect."

"That's why I thought I should keep quiet today. It allowed Debbie to have her say and that's how it should've been."

"Good idea. Everything worked out well. Mind you, I was a little shocked that they thought we might be forcing Debbie to stay."

Cherish grimaced when she saw how sweetly her mother smiled at Levi.

Wilma then continued, "I'm just thinking that it's so hard for Debbie. She is such a gentle soul and doesn't want to upset anybody. I'm glad she stayed strong. I do believe that staying here will be the best thing for her."

"Of course it will," said Levi.

"Well there's not much we can do about the name. Debbie is not going to go back on that. I was a little surprised that she said what she said."

Levi looked up from his reading. "What did she say?"

"She said something about the marriage being unconventional so she did something unconventional with the name."

Levi chuckled. "I do remember that, but when Cherish said something about that, you growled at her."

"I had to. I didn't want her to be pleased that the Bontragers were upset."

"I don't think she was. She was just pleased that Debbie was starting to stand up for herself."

Cherish was delighted that Levi saw things the same way as she did.

Mamm continued, "If she wasn't pleased at their misfortune then what I said wouldn't upset her much. Not that it probably upset her at all. You know how thin-skinned she is."

"Do you mean thick-skinned?"

"That's right, thick-skinned. Nothing bothers that girl."

"It's going to be quiet around here when you're at the farm. How long will you be gone?"

"Just a few days. A week at the most. I don't like to be gone too long. Debbie needs me. Bliss also needs me with this dreadful ordeal happening with Adam. I do hope that's resolved soon. The girl's at the breaking point."

"Maybe Adam isn't the right one for her," Levi said.

"Of course he is. Do you know anyone better suited? Because I don't."

87

"No, but she's only young. She'll find someone eventually. It's no shame for a woman to get married later in life, you know. We married each other and we weren't exactly young."

Wilma grumbled. "Only a man would say that. Anyway, this is our second marriage for both of us."

"I mean it, Wilma, these things shouldn't be rushed. You said so yourself when you came back from visiting Mercy and Honor."

"I know, but we're talking about Adam and Bliss. I wasn't worried about Bliss rushing into something, I was worried about Cherish and Favor. I don't mind if they take their time. And Bliss can rush if she's rushing with Adam."

Levi raised his eyebrows and continued reading.

Cherish got up when nothing more was said, and headed back to bed. Once she was in bed, she moved her dog over to one side so she had room to stretch out. Her heavy eyelids closed thinking about what Favor had said about John. None of the Bakers had even met him and yet he was affecting all their lives. She knew that was profound in some way, but before she could think it through, her eyelids grew heavy and sleep overtook her.

CHAPTER 16

On the day of the tea testing, Matthew met Debbie, Favor, Bliss and Cherish at the farmers market. He was bringing a trestle table. Cherish walked over to help him lift the table out of the back of the buggy.

"I've been waiting to see you again," Cherish told him.

His face lit up. "I've been waiting to see you, too."

"Good. So you've thought of a plan to get Adam and Bliss back together?"

"No. I forgot all about it. I thought you meant you were just pleased to see me."

Cherish made a face. "Seriously?"

He nodded.

"Matthew, I was relying on you."

"I'm sorry. I've been thinking about my future here. That's what I've been thinking about. Forgive me for being selfish. I'll come up with something."

Cherish grunted, "That's what you said a couple of days ago."

"Just trust me." He took the blanket off the table. They carried it to the entrance and placed it where Debbie directed them. Then they started setting up the tea.

A man walked past, but not before having a good look at them and what they were doing. Then he walked back to them. "Do you have a permit?" he asked Matthew.

Matthew stared at him. "I'm sorry, but who are you?"

"I'm a stallholder. I have a market stall that I pay for. No one's allowed to sell out here."

Matthew looked over at Debbie who was arranging her tea. "Hey, Debbie, do we have a permit?"

Debbie looked up. "For what?"

"To be here," the stallholder replied.

"No. Do we need one?"

"Of course you do. You just can't come here and start selling your goods. We all need to pay."

Cherish stepped up. "We're not selling anything. We're just testing samples for public opinions. We'll only be here for a couple of hours. Or maybe just one hour."

He frowned and then murmured that they'd still probably need a permit, and then he walked inside the building.

"Are we in trouble?" Debbie asked.

"Just ignore him. I think we only need a permit if we're selling things," Favor said.

Debbie looked around. "I hope you're right."

"We won't be here long, will we?" Matthew asked. "How many people do we need to taste the tea?"

Debbie bit her lip. That was something she couldn't answer. She didn't recall how many she might need or whether her unofficial tea-making-mentor had even mentioned a number. "I don't know."

Matthew tipped his hat back on his head. "Ten, thirty, one hundred?"

"I think it only needs to be small. The main thing is that the people don't know us. We've only got enough hot water for fifty."

"Okay. People are starting to arrive now. Have we got the tea ready yet, Debbie?"

"It'll be set up in a minute." They had a portable gas burner to heat the water.

As Cherish helped out, she thought about the first time they were supposed to do this, when Simon said he'd come to meet her. She was a little surprised that so many of her thoughts were taken up by Simon.

Being at the farmers market reminded Bliss of Adam. But then again, everything reminded her of Adam. How would she go on without him? Her life was ruined.

Favor was pleased to be out of the house, away from the orchard. She was getting out of chores and for that, she was grateful.

When the samples were mostly all gone, Debbie became more withdrawn. It had been hard to get people to stop a moment and try out the tea. They did, once they were told it was free. The feedback wasn't great.

People weren't enthusiastic about the tea.

Cherish's heart was breaking for Debbie. Why were people being so mean?

Just when she was going to give up and go home, someone arrived that Debbie knew. It was Fredrick

Lomas, the man who owned the tea packaging and sales business.

"Fredrick, what are you doing here?" Debbie was embarrassed that people weren't raving about her tea. Now Fredrick would find out.

"I heard a whisper you'd be here. Mind if I try your tea?"

"I'd be honored if you would." Debbie took a sample cup and gave him the rose and pomegranate. He swallowed and moved his lips around as he tasted it. "What do you think?" Debbie asked.

He looked at her, then looked back down at the samples. "I'll try the lemon and hibiscus." She passed it to him and he took a sip. "What are people saying about this one?" he asked.

"I'm not sure yet. We haven't looked at what they've written down. I was going to do that when I got home. What do you think?"

"I think the flavor isn't coming through enough."

"Oh. What can I do?"

"Have a look at your feedback and if you're not happy, bring all the comments and your tea to me, and I'll see if I can help you adjust your formulas."

"You'd do that?" Debbie asked.

"Sure. I'd like to see you succeed."

"Thank you."

"You've got my number."

"I do."

"Call me and we'll make a time." He looked at the pages and said, "Is that how many people have sampled the tea?"

"Yes."

He picked up the pages, and flipped through them. "This is enough."

"Is it?" Debbie asked.

"Yes."

"Great. Thank you. I'll be in touch."

He nodded and then moved away.

"Was that your tea man?" Favor asked.

"Yes. Let's pack up. I won't look at what people said until I get home. I don't think people liked the tea as much as I hoped they would."

"Don't worry until you see what all the people said."

Debbie didn't say anything, but she had seen from the looks on their faces that most of them weren't impressed.

Matthew whispered to Cherish, "She's upset."

The manager of the farmers market walked up as they were packing up. "Who's in charge here?"

Cherish recognized him and stepped forward. She knew him from a few years ago when she and her sisters had a stall. "Hello, Mr. Pettigrew. I'm Cherish Baker. "

He looked at her with no recognition in his eyes.

Cherish continued, "My family had a stall here for a couple of years."

"Then you should know that what you're doing is not allowed." He pointed at the table.

"We're just leaving and besides, we weren't selling anything."

His eyebrows drew together. "What were you doing?"

Debbie stepped forward. "I'm sorry. This was my fault. We were taste-testing my tea. We needed a cross-section of people who didn't know us to use as a focus group."

His face got softer as he smiled at Debbie. "Still, it's questionable with my insurance and whether they'd cover any one of you who were illegally operating here."

"I'm sorry. We didn't know we were doing anything wrong."

Matthew said, "It was my fault. I suggested we come here because of all the people who'd be here. What do we owe you, moneywise, for setting up here?"

Cherish was pleased Matthew was taking control. He was acting like a real man and not the boy he acted like most of the time.

Mr. Pettigrew shook his head. "Just don't do it again unless you ask. I could've found some space for you inside, Mrs. ...?"

"Mrs. ... Ms. Bruner."

He nodded and then looked up at the sky. "Seems it's going to rain. The forecast is for a thunderstorm."

Cherish was quick to say, "We better get out of here before we get caught in the downpour."

Mr. Pettigrew gave a nod before he left them and walked into the building.

"That was a close call," Matthew said.

"Thanks, Matthew, but I think this was my idea. You didn't need to take the blame."

"I thought it would be better if he talked to another man. Men can talk reasonably to each other."

Favor sniggered. "Yeah, you did a great job, Matthew."

"You sure did," Debbie agreed. "I thought we might have to pay for a moment."

"Do you even have any money?" Cherish asked him.

"No. Not on me. Let's pack this up before we get caught in the rain."

Debbie was grateful to have so many helpers, but she knew she wouldn't feel as good when she looked at the results of the survey.

CHAPTER 17

*D*ebbie had been right. She sat down in the living room with Ada on one side and Wilma on the other as she read aloud what people had written about her tea.

Debbie read out the last two of the comments. "Not enough flavor. Here's another one. It tasted like dishwater. The only one that was popular was the lemon tea. I thought that was the boring one. Anyone can make lemon tea."

"Maybe these people weren't telling the truth," Ada suggested.

"They had no reason to lie. They don't know me and I don't know them."

"That is unusual. We like all your tea. Just sell the lemon tea, then," Wilma suggested.

"If I'm to make a real go of this, I'll need more than one flavor. Fredrick said he'd help me with the recipes."

"That's *wunderbaar*. And he's an expert, you say?" Wilma asked.

97

"He is. He knows so much about tea. I think he knows everything."

Ada patted Debbie's arm. *"Gott* has sent him to guide you."

"I agree. I need some guidance. I just feel so disappointed with these results."

"Don't be upset," Ada told her. "Everyone has to start somewhere. And if these opinions are true, it would've been wrong for you to put so much effort into something when you could've had better tea."

"I know. You're right. That's what Fredrick said. I have to sort out my flavors first."

"And that's what you're doing. I'm proud of you, Debbie."

Debbie turned to look at Wilma. "You are?"

"I am. You've had so many problems and mountains to climb and then you bounce back and start thinking about something other than your own problems. I'm sure you'll do well out of this."

"I hope so. I thought about giving up, but I'll keep going. I'm really enjoying it."

"What does Peter White think about you making tea?" Ada asked.

"He's so supportive. He's the one that took me to the tea factory in the first place."

"Ah, that's right. I did forget that."

Debbie straightened up all her pieces of paper. "Before I started today, I thought everyone would love my tea."

"We do."

"I know, but most people don't."

Wilma put her hand on Debbie's arm. "This is the first

rung on the ladder. Get that right and then you climb onto the next rung. Pretty soon you'll be up at the top."

"Thanks for all your encouragement, Aunt Wilma. It means a lot. You too, Ada."

Ada smiled, and said, "You'll always have our support."

CHAPTER 18

The next morning, it was Cherish's turn to take some meals over to Christina. She pushed Christina's front door open. "Hello."

"I'm in the bedroom."

Cherish left the casserole dish on the kitchen counter and then walked into the bedroom. One twin was on the bed, making small crying noises while Christina was changing the other twin's diaper.

Christina looked like she'd had a bit more sleep. She was fully dressed and the bed was even made. "Hi, Cherish, thanks for coming over."

"I left a meal in the kitchen."

"Great. The food has been such a big help."

"Good."

"Do you want to change a diaper?"

Cherish made a face. "No. I don't know how. I've never had much to do with babies."

Christina laughed. "I don't think that's entirely true. What about Faith and also Iris?"

Cherish smiled. "Well, I haven't changed Iris's diaper."

"So you do know how?" Christina asked.

"A little bit. Okay, I'll change her." Cherish found a diaper and set about changing the other baby.

Once the babies were changed, Christina put them into their shared crib for a nap.

Cherish looked over at the second crib. "I rushed out and got that second crib. Do you think you'll ever use it?"

"Of course. When they're bigger." Christina closed the door on them.

"Should I go? Do you want to get some sleep?"

"No, I'll be fine. Let's sit on the couch. I haven't had anyone to talk to for a while. As soon as Mark comes home, I'll get some sleep."

"Okay. I've got plenty of time." They both sat on the couch.

Christina said, "I had a good night last night. They both slept for five hours. I think I'll be able to go to the meeting next Sunday."

"That's great. Everyone will be so excited to see the babies."

"How's Bliss doing?"

"Just the same. Nothing has changed at all. I tried to get her to come with me, but she said she'd come next time. She's just so depressed. Things didn't go well the last time Bliss went somewhere with me." Cherish told Christina how cold Adam had acted when Bliss literally ran into him.

"It's hard for her, but everything will work out."

"How do you know?" Cherish asked.

"It always does. Everything works out for the best. Just

look at my two babies. I had pain and heartache for many years and now I have two miracles."

Cherish couldn't deny that. Christina's babies were a true miracle. And that gave Cherish more faith to believe in miracles and to believe that God is a God who answers prayers. "It's true, but it's hard for Bliss because she's going through it now. It was hard for you before your babies arrived, before you got pregnant."

"Oh yes, I know what you mean. I was destroyed every day. Half the time I doubted that *Gott* was even there. Doubted that He was even listening to my pleas and my cries. He did, and He won't be any different with Bliss or anyone else."

"I can see that that's true. Maybe Bliss should talk to you."

"Of course. She was over here the other day, but she didn't say much."

"I think she's trying to put on a brave face in front of other people. She probably wouldn't want to tell you how she really feels. But if you ask her questions, she might open up to you."

"I'll do that."

"Thank you. Are the twins identical?"

"I believe so, but I can tell them apart."

"How?"

"There's a slight difference in the width of the forehead and their temperaments are different too. One is far more relaxed and the other is a little more uptight."

"It's interesting that they can have personalities right from the start."

"Everyone is born with their own personalities. I believe that."

"I wonder how many more babies you'll have."

Christina smiled widely. "As many as *Gott* gives us. We didn't start off young, but these twins have given us a good head start."

"I think having twins is a good idea. Only one pregnancy and one birth and then you have the two-in-one package. Two for the price of one." Cherish giggled.

"There's more work involved with twins, but I think it will be easier once they get older."

They heard scratching sounds at the door. "What's that?" Christina asked.

"That will be Caramel. He's got out of the buggy. I told him to stay there. He's a naughty dog sometimes. I should go now anyway." Cherish jumped up and Christina walked her to the door.

"Tell Wilma thanks for the food. It has been convenient having the food ready. We are very appreciative of all the help your mother has given us, and Ada, too, of course."

"Yeah, they're not bad for a couple of old ducks."

"Oh, Cherish." Christina laughed. "Whatever you do, don't let them hear you say that."

"I'm not *that* silly."

"Say goodbye to the twins for me. "

"I will."

"Do you have any names yet? Everyone's anxiously waiting for the names."

Christina shook her head. "We've got a short list. We'll most likely decide later today."

"I can't wait to hear what they are." Cherish walked out the door and Caramel jumped up on her, putting his muddy paws all over her white apron. "Get down. And get back into the buggy. See what you've done, Caramel?"

"That's why we don't have a dog." Christina laughed.

"You don't have a dog yet, but I'm sure the twins would like a puppy when they're older."

"Hmm, we'll see."

"That was a mother's response. You're learning already. *Mamm* always says 'we'll see' when she means no." Cherish gave Christina a sideways hug goodbye, careful not to get any dirt on her.

On the drive home, Cherish slowed down when she got to Eddie, the beekeeper's property, as she always did. She couldn't believe it when she saw Gertie's buggy there again. That meant Krystal was visiting. Again. She didn't have a buggy of her own and she used Gertie's.

"What's really going on between those two?" Cherish said out loud.

It wasn't right for a newly Amish woman, for that matter *any* Amish woman to keep visiting an *Englisher*.

Cherish slowed the buggy even more.

Should she confront them again? She'd done that last time and it seemed that Krystal didn't give two hoots about being caught alone with Eddie.

Then Cherish had a thought. If Krystal kept herself busy by visiting Eddie, she'd leave Adam alone.

Cherish moved the buggy forward, hoping that might be true.

CHAPTER 19

The day before Fairfax and Hope were due to arrive home from visiting relatives, Wilma had an idea. "Hope will be back tomorrow. It would be nice if you girls clean the cottage so it's ready for their return."

Cherish was chewing on a chocolate cookie and she stopped as soon as she heard her mother's suggestion. "I'm busy doing things."

"Me too," Favor said. "Besides, Hope said they're moving into the big house. It'd be a complete waste to clean up the cottage."

Ada butted in as she so often did, "What your mother meant to say was one, two, three of you," she pointed at Bliss, Favor, and Cherish in turn, "will stop what you're doing and go over there right now to clean the house and make it look nice for their return. Perhaps you could add some flowers to the kitchen table."

"We have no flowers in the garden at this time of year," Favor said.

"Well, just clean the place and make it look nice." Ada gave a nod at her suggestion.

The girls all stood up. "You want us to go now, *Mamm?*" Favor asked.

"Yes I do."

The girls walked out of the kitchen to get their coats.

"See, Wilma? That's how it's done." Ada and Wilma put their heads together and chuckled.

"This is a crazy idea." Favor stomped through the orchard on her way to Fairfax and Hope's cottage.

Bliss said, "It will be nice for them to come home to a clean place. They left so soon after the wedding so they might not have had much time to concentrate on their place."

Favor glared at Bliss. "You're always agreeing with *Mamm.*"

Cherish poked Favor in her side so Bliss wouldn't see. Any little comment was likely to set Bliss off in tears again.

Favor glanced at Cherish, and caught on to what Cherish was thinking. "I'm sorry, both of you," Favor said. "I'm just grumpy today, that's all."

"There's a lot of that going around," said Cherish. "But with the three of us, we'll get this done in no time. It's probably not even dirty. You know what Hope's like, she's forever cleaning things."

"That's true," Favor said.

When they got to the front door of the cottage, Favor retrieved the key from under the mat. As soon as they let themselves in, they noticed the brand new furniture.

"Wow, this is all so nice," Bliss ran her hands along the bleached wooden dining table.

Favor turned around in a circle. "And the place looks clean enough to me."

The girls then moved to the small kitchen. On the floor in the corner were wedding presents. Some were opened and some unopened.

Cherish picked up a wrapped gift and shook it. "Perhaps we can open some wedding presents."

Bliss giggled. "I think they'd be pretty mad if we did that."

"I guess so."

Favor said, "I can't wait till I get married. I can get some awesome presents."

Cherish rolled her eyes at Favor's comment. Anything could set Bliss off crying again, especially any talk of weddings or anything to do with weddings or marriage. "You get presents all the time for Christmas and birthdays."

"I know, but for weddings people give you better presents."

Bliss moved away. "I'll look in the other rooms to see where to start first."

Cherish moved closer to Favor, and hissed, "Will you stop talking about wedding stuff?"

Favor placed her hands on her hips. "It's a bit hard at the moment. That's why we're here. Hope's just gotten married so it's hard not to talk about it."

Bliss walked back into the room, looking like she was about to burst into tears. "I heard what you both said. "I'll never get any wedding presents now that I'm never going to marry."

Cherish was fumingly mad. "Good work, Favor," she blurted out.

"It's your fault. You wanted to open the presents, not me. You started it."

"No *you* started it." Cherish jabbed a finger through the air, pointing at Favor.

"So I should just continue my life having to watch what I say?" Favor's voice rose, which made it even more high-pitched sounding than normal. Cherish covered her ears.

Bliss sighed. "Stop it both of you. You're both making me feel worse."

Favor took a step closer to Bliss. "You'll forget about Adam soon. Don't worry."

"Thanks, but I doubt it. Well, where should we start? We're here for a reason. I don't want to think about Adam right now." Bliss looked around.

Cherish poked one of the wrapped wedding gifts. Favor slapped her hand away.

"Ouch."

"We're here to clean," Favor groused at Cherish.

"I don't see why. It looks clean to me."

Bliss said, "The kitchen needs a wipe over."

"We'll start in the kitchen then," Cherish said. "And, we'll wipe it over."

"That won't need three of us. I'll sweep the floor," Favor volunteered.

Bliss suggested Cherish should clean the windows.

Then all three went their separate ways.

An hour later when they were ready to go, Favor said, "I really don't know how Hope had the time to have the place so nice before she left. The place was already clean."

Cherish said, "Don't you remember, she wasn't at our place much the day before she left. She came back here to clean. She should've been at home, cleaning up. It was her wedding after all."

Bliss agreed. "That's true, but it doesn't matter. We've done all we can. Now we can leave."

Cherish took a last look at the presents. "Can't I just have a little peek? It wouldn't hurt if I just lifted up a little of the paper and had a look inside. I can stick it back down again."

"No," Bliss and Favor said at the same time.

"What about just one of them?" Cherish asked.

"No," came the resounding reply from Favor.

"Unfair." Cherish pouted as she looked at the gifts. She had an overwhelming urge to know what was inside and didn't know why Bliss and Favor didn't feel the same.

Bliss took one last look around. "I do wish we could've had some nice flowers like Ada suggested. It would be a nice surprise when they come home."

"Where are we going to get flowers from at this late notice?" Favor asked. "Nowhere, that's where."

Bliss sat down on the couch. "I don't mean to depress everybody, but it's a bit sad for me being here." Bliss's bottom lip wobbled. "Hope has her husband. I thought I would be next in line to marry out of all of us."

"And you still might," Cherish said, quite forgetting she wasn't going to give her any false hope.

Favor sat down next to Bliss. "That's right, you might.

He's got to realize how silly he is sooner or later. You're the most perfect woman for him. I mean, no one is as nice or as kind as you are, Bliss."

Bliss wiped a tear from her eye. "I'm sorry. I don't mean to be like this, but I can't stop feeling so sad. It's like there is no color in my world now. Everything is just blah without Adam. I loved spending time with him. And when I wasn't with him, I was thinking about him."

Favor looked up at Cherish, wanting her to say something to make Bliss feel better, but there was nothing she could say. She'd run out of encouragement and so, it seemed, had Favor.

Bliss wiped away some tears and stood up. "I'll get past this."

"Of course you will," said Favor.

"I agree," said Cherish.

"Let's go."

They locked up and replaced the key, and the three of them walked back through the orchard. All the way back home, Cherish prayed that Matthew would come up with a good plan or at least have had a good conversation with Andrew about Adam. Surely there would be something lurking in Adam's past to make him see that he wasn't perfect. That was the only thing Cherish could think of to get them back together.

CHAPTER 20

*a*fter dinner that night, Cherish pulled Matthew aside in the corner of the living room. There was nowhere else to have a private talk since it was too cold outside on the porch.

"I've been trusting you, Matthew. What have you come up with?"

"I decided I will talk with Andrew."

"I thought we'd already decided that you would."

Matthew opened his mouth to speak, but Cherish kept talking.

"And what will you say?"

"I'll just start a conversation about Adam and Bliss and see what he says."

"Don't make it obvious."

"I won't. I'll just try and lead the conversation in that direction."

Cherish nodded. "Okay, that sounds good."

"Trust me, I'm good at talking."

"I really think it would be a good idea to find out about

Adam's history, but I have no idea how to do that because he's not from this community. And I don't know any way I can find anyone who knows him without Bliss or Adam finding out what we're up to."

"Leave it with me. I know what I'm doing."

Cherish smiled. "Thanks, Matthew. I knew I could rely on you."

He smiled back at her. "Always."

"But don't let me down."

"I won't."

"I really hope something works or Bliss will be sad forever. Everyone says she'll get over it, but what if she doesn't?"

"She'll get over it as soon as she finds someone else. That is, if they don't get back together."

"That won't be easy if she has to find someone else because Adam is pretty amazing."

Matthew cleared his throat. "I know, you keep reminding me. Looks aren't everything."

"I didn't say they were."

"I didn't say you did, but I do think you think that to a degree."

Cherish scrunched up her face. "What are you talking about? I never said anything of the kind."

"Maybe not, but you did list that as one of Adam's attributes."

"It doesn't hurt that he looks nice, but Bliss is in love with him not for the way he looks, he's got other things about him. He started his own business and it's going really, really well. That means he'll be able to provide Bliss with a house and everything she'll ever need. And they won't have money worries when they have children to feed. That is, if your plan works."

Matthew rubbed his forehead. "So their future depends on me?"

"It does."

"Thanks a lot."

"Well I can't do anything, because I'm going to the farm soon."

"I'll do my best. That's all I can do."

"That's all I'm asking. When will you do it?"

"When the time's right." Matthew moved away and joined the others.

Cherish stood there, staring after him. 'When the time's right?' That didn't sit well with Cherish. To her, everything should be done immediately, especially with how much Bliss was suffering.

The right time was right now! Well, at least tomorrow.

CHAPTER 21

The next day, Hope burst into the house through the back door. "We're back!" Fairfax walked in after her. The whole family was sitting down eating lunch. Ada and Samuel were there too, along with Matthew.

"Has it been two and a half weeks already?" *Mamm* asked as though she wasn't expecting them.

"Yes, it has." Hope hugged her mother. "Was someone at the cottage while we were away?"

Ada said, "Your sisters were kind enough to make sure it was nice for you."

"Thanks so much. It was lovely to get home and for everything to be so clean. We left in such a hurry."

"I hope you're all ready to get going with work." Fairfax rubbed his hands together, looking at all the girls.

"It's winter. There's not much to do." Favor then looked at him. "Since we're the owners of the orchard, you work for us, don't you, Fairfax?"

Cherish was surprised she'd say such a thing, but it

was true.

"If you want to get technical, I work for Florence. Since you've all agreed to work under Florence, that would mean you've agreed to work under me, which means I'm your boss."

Favor looked down, while Ada chuckled.

Fairfax continued, "There are always things to do in the orchard. We can check the fences, check the trees and then we can keep the equipment in good order. Even though the trees seem to be asleep, they're not asleep and neither should we sleep."

"Aren't you also looking after your parents' old orchard and Florence's orchard, too?" Wilma asked.

"That's right."

"That'll keep you busy."

Fairfax chuckled. "I don't mind being busy."

"How was everyone back at home?" Matthew asked.

"I was just about to tell everyone that, Matthew. You got in before me." Hope said, "They're fine. The boys are adorable and the babies are growing so fast."

"I wish I could've gone with you," Favor moaned. "It's not fair."

"There will be other times," *Mamm* said.

"No there won't. It'll be other people going and not me. I never get to go anywhere."

"It's a long way away. Perhaps they'll come for a visit," Cherish suggested.

"No they won't. They didn't come for Hope's wedding."

"That's only because their children are too young."

"Yeah, and next time their excuse will be something

else. They'll probably have more babies by then and they'll be too young."

"Hush, Favor. I haven't finished telling everyone my news."

Everyone made room at the table for Hope and Fairfax. While Hope told them everything they did while they were away, Bliss sat there thinking about Adam. She had thought she'd be the next one married after Hope—and thought she'd be married to Adam. Now she wouldn't have the next wedding in the family. That thought wouldn't stop playing over and over in her mind.

It was hard for Bliss to focus on anything other than her problems with Adam and all the what ifs. What if Krystal planned to take advantage of the situation? If Adam and Krystal started dating, it would be the most awful thing ever. Everyone knew Krystal had always had her eyes on Adam. And if he did date Krystal, it wouldn't be fair. He wasn't forgiving her for a past mistake, but what about all the mistakes Krystal had made in her life?

"Anyway, what's been happening here? What have we missed?" Hope asked.

"Nothing much," *Mamm* said.

"I'll have to see Mark and Christina's babies. I can't wait."

"I can take you there tomorrow if you want," Bliss said.

"Okay. I'd love that."

Cherish added, "We had people test Debbie's teas to see if they liked them. That was such fun."

Debbie looked down. "It didn't go so well."

"Why? What happened?" Hope asked.

119

"They liked the lemon tea, but hardly anyone liked the others. I'm having someone help me with the recipes. I'm going to play around with them tonight to see what I can come up with."

Matthew laughed. "While we were there, we got into trouble with the manager of the markets."

Ada gasped. "No one told me that."

"I wasn't told either," Wilma said. "It's nothing to laugh about, Matthew. We can't get a bad name around town."

"It was no problem. It wasn't a big deal. He was nice. He said if he'd known we were coming, he would've found us a place inside."

"Yeah, it was no problem," Favor said.

"I hope not. The last thing we want is for us to get a bad name just like Wilma said," Ada told Matthew.

Mamm continued, "We're well respected around town and I don't want anything to change that."

"It won't change, Wilma. It was really okay. Everything was fine."

Wilma stared at Matthew. "I'll have to take your word on that. But you should've asked if you could've set up there, in the parking lot."

"It was my fault. I'm sorry, Aunt Wilma, I just wasn't thinking." Debbie shook her head.

"It's okay. You've had a lot on your mind. You can't be expected to think of everything when you're concentrating on your tea."

Samuel said, "I'm sure Hope and Fairfax want to tell us more about their time away."

Then Hope took over the conversation and told them

about every place they'd visited.

THAT NIGHT, Bliss burst into Cherish's room. Cherish was just settling into bed. Bliss hurried to sit on her bedside. "I need to talk to you about something."

Cherish hoped she hadn't found out that Matthew was going to talk with Andrew. "What is it?" Cherish sat up.

"I need you to find out how close Krystal and Adam are."

"Me?"

"Yes. I know we broke up but he doesn't have to ignore me completely. We are in the same community. I'm wondering if he's acting so distant because he's guilty. That's why I need you to find out if there's something going on. You and I both know that Krystal has always liked him."

"How will I do that?" Cherish gulped.

"Ask her."

Cherish rubbed her head. She didn't want to be anywhere near Krystal. "You want me to go to the quilt shop?"

"Great idea."

Cherish rolled her eyes.

Bliss's mouth turned down at the corners. "Well, you don't have to do it."

Cherish knew she had to do it. "I'll go if that's what you want. What will I say I'm there for?"

"Just make up something."

Cherish yawned and then covered her mouth. "I could

say I'm looking at the patterns again."

"You could take *Mamm* with you."

"Are you crazy? Why would I do that?"

"She might like to spend time with you and she'd be more willing for you to leave the house."

"Or I could go there after I finish work. You pick me up tomorrow when I finish and drive me there. My shift finishes at three and her shop will still be open. You can park up the road so she doesn't see you."

Bliss thought about that for a while and then slowly nodded. "Okay."

"Why are you worried about Krystal? Have you heard something?" Cherish asked.

"Only that he's doing some work in the quilt shop."

"I told you that."

Bliss shrugged her shoulders. "That's the only thing I've heard. I need more information and I don't know how else to get it."

Cherish knew this wouldn't help toward getting Bliss and Adam back together, but she couldn't say no to Bliss. "I'll do what I can."

Bliss threw her arms around her neck. "Thanks, Cherish."

Cherish giggled. "Don't thank me now. I don't even know if I'll find anything out."

"I know, but I feel I have to do something. I can't sit around and do nothing."

How could Cherish tell Bliss not to get her hopes up? Cherish felt she had no reason to bring her down. Maybe Levi was right and in time, Bliss would forget about Adam.

CHAPTER 22

*A*s arranged, Bliss picked up Cherish from the café after she'd finished for the day.

"So what's the plan?" Cherish asked as she climbed into the buggy.

"Same as we agreed on last night. Just go to the quilt store and look around then get talking to Krystal. If something's going on, she won't be able to keep quiet about it."

"It's far too early for anything to be going on."

"No it's not. She'd swoop in on him. She'll see the opportunity and she'll go for it. You know what she's like."

Cherish faced the front. Yes, she knew what Krystal was like in regards to men. Like a hawk who sees a young chick who strayed too far from it's mother.

"How was your day?" Bliss asked.

"Good. I wish I could work there every day."

Bliss grunted. "No point even thinking about that. I

can't believe they let you and they won't let me work there."

"It's *Mamm*, I think. Levi has the final say over you. *Mamm* must want me out of the house." Cherish giggled. "She might need a break from me. Weren't you going to ask Levi again if you can work at the café?"

"I was, but I haven't yet. Do you really think he'll let me?"

"If you say it'll make you feel better he might."

"I'll ask him. I'll wait until he's in the right mood. Now when you get to the quilt shop, don't be obvious about why you're there. If Krystal thinks you're there for information she'll clam up and won't tell you anything."

"I doubt there's anything to tell." Cherish felt sorry for Bliss. She was going to get upset when Adam started dating. It wouldn't matter if it was with Krystal or anyone else. There was no point to this, but Bliss was acting like an obsessed crazy person.

Bliss drove the long way so she wouldn't drive past the quilt store, then she parked up the road.

"Park closer. This is such a long way to walk."

"I can't. There are no closer parking spots, and if I'm closer, Krystal might see me. Don't be lazy. Walking is good for you."

Cherish got out, crossed the road and started toward the quilt store. She didn't like Bliss's comment just now about being lazy. She wasn't lazy so why did everyone call her that? It was annoying. Was Bliss becoming like the rest of them? What if she spent more time with Ada and *Mamm* and became just like them? Even more reason to get her and Adam back together.

Looking in the shop window, Cherish saw there were no customers. Krystal was sitting at the back, behind the computer. Cherish took a deep breath and walked up the front step and into the store.

Krystal looked up, seeming surprised. "Cherish. Are you here alone?"

"Yes. I just finished my shift at the café."

"Ah, you could've brought me a coffee. I was just thinking I could do with one right now. I can make one myself in the back, but it's not the same as from a café."

"I didn't think of it, sorry. If I'd known I was coming here I would've."

Krystal looked her up and down. "Why are you here? Have you changed your mind about buying one of the quilts?"

Cherish looked around. "Just checking on the quilt patterns again. It's the best way to see them all in one place."

"Didn't your mother already decide on a pattern?"

"Yes, but you know what she's like—always thinking ahead to the next project." Cherish kept looking around.

"How many do you guys plan to make?"

"Quite a few. It'll be an ongoing thing. This next one's for Hope and then it'll be Joy and then... I don't know."

"Bliss? Or are you doing them for when your sisters get married. Bliss won't be the next one like everyone thought. Isn't that the truth?"

The last thing Cherish wanted was to agree with her. "Who knows? They just have to work out their differences. I think they're getting there."

Krystal's eyes grew wide. "Really?"

"Absolutely."

"That's not the impression I got when Adam was here recently."

"What did he say?"

Krystal smirked, like she had a secret. "I don't like to repeat things told to me in confidence."

"He told you something in confidence?" Cherish asked.

"That's right."

"I don't believe you. He wouldn't have said anything to you."

"Believe what you want." Krystal straightened a price tag on one of the quilts. "He's doing some work here soon so we will be able to display the quilts better."

"Anyway, I didn't come here to talk about Bliss and Adam. How are things with you?"

"Great. I sold two quilts yesterday and one this morning. Also, one over the internet."

"That's great. You're doing really well."

"I know. And I love it. I'm helping two other businesses get their things on the internet. I told Adam I could help his business too."

"What did he say about that?"

"He said he's busy enough and if he got busier he'd have to employ more people. He's not ready to do that right now. How's Bliss doing? I suppose she's very upset over Adam breaking up with her."

Cherish's mouth turned down at the corners. "Why do you assume he was the one who ended it?"

Krystal cackled. "Who would break up with Adam?

Any girl would be mad to do that. Besides, everyone knows what happened."

"What does everyone know?" Cherish hoped no one knew about Bliss writing to John. Ada knew and obviously Matthew had found out somehow, but they were the only ones outside the family who knew.

"I don't know the nitty gritty details if that's what you mean. So is Bliss upset?" Krystal asked.

"No. She's not upset at all. She's perfectly fine."

"But they've broken up for sure, haven't they?" Krystal took a step closer to Cherish.

Cherish was pleased that she didn't know what was going on. That told her nothing was happening between Krystal and Adam.

"I'm not sure. I don't like to ask too many questions. I don't like being nosy." Cherish did a full circle and looked at each of the quilts again. Then she spun around. "Thanks for letting me look around."

"I can't charge you for looking. If I could, I would."

Cherish laughed. "Have you seen Eddie lately?"

The smile left Krystal's face. "No. Why would I?"

"Just asking the question."

"I know what you think you saw a few weeks ago, but there's nothing between us. His family was good to me, and that's all. Don't start rumors. I don't want to have problems with the bishop. He's been really good to me about allowing me to leave the Millers' dairy farm."

Cherish wasn't ready to let it go. "So you were so close to Eddie in his shed because you were thanking him about something? Or... what was the reason?"

Krystal opened her mouth in shock. "I'm not sure what you think you saw, but you're wrong."

Cherish shrugged her shoulders. "Okay."

"You are wrong, Cherish. It's not what you think... or thought."

"I said okay. I don't really care anyway."

"Then why did you bring it up?"

"I was only being polite. Look, there's no reason that we shouldn't get along," Cherish said.

Krystal stared at her for a moment. "There is a reason why we've never gotten along. You don't like me and you never have. You've never been nice to me from the start."

"I can't believe you're saying that right now. It's you who hasn't liked me from the start. All I wanted to say is that we should try to get along."

"We should, but will we?" Krystal asked.

"We could try," Cherish said. "I'm willing."

Krystal nodded. "Okay. If you try, I'll try, but it doesn't help when you keep saying things to upset me."

"What, like ask if you've seen Eddie?"

Krystal nodded.

"Okay. I will never ask about Eddie again," Cherish said.

"Good." Krystal smiled.

"I should go. Next time I'll bring you a take-out coffee."

"Thank you. That would be nice. I'm here most days."

"Noted. Bye, Krystal."

After Krystal said goodbye, Cherish walked out of the shop, feeling stirred up. It was never nice to talk with

Krystal, but hopefully they'd just made some kind of truce. As she walked toward the buggy, she turned back around and saw Krystal staring after her.

Krystal was looking past her, up the street at the horse and buggy.

Cherish knew she would've been able to see Bliss in the driver's seat.

"Oh no, She saw me," Bliss said, when Cherish got back into the buggy.

"I know."

Bliss stared at Cherish. "Did you tell her I was here?"

"Of course not. But she doesn't know you weren't taking care of something else and meeting me here. Right?"

"That's true." Bliss moved the buggy onward. Now, it didn't matter if they drove past the store. "What did she say?"

"She didn't really know the situation between you and Adam. That tells me they can't be close. I wouldn't worry about her if I were you. He is going to do some work in the quilt store. I'm not sure when, but you can't let yourself worry about all that. He could date anyone, not only her."

Bliss stared at her, taking her eyes off the road for a moment. "Thanks. That makes me feel a whole lot better," she said sarcastically. "Now I'm having visions of a line of women waiting to date him."

"That's not what I meant at all. There's no line of women. I just don't want you to worry about Krystal. He's clearly not interested in her and she didn't even try to make out there was something going on, even to annoy me."

Bliss sighed. "I can't do anything about anyone he dates. You're right. I don't know what to do. I wish I could travel back in time. I would've avoided John Bontrager and never written back to him. I didn't even know Adam when I first wrote to John."

"John's had a huge impact on Debbie and now you. Debbie probably wishes she had avoided him too, but then she never would've had Jared and I'm sure she wouldn't want that. I wouldn't want that either. He's part of our family now."

"I feel so helpless and hopeless. Have you ever felt like that?"

Cherish nodded. "Most days."

A glimmer of a smile hinted around Bliss's lips. "Don't make me laugh. I don't want to be happy. I'm too sad to be happy."

Cherish sat there in silence because she didn't know what to say. She couldn't comfort her and tell her that Adam would change his mind in case he never did. Normally, Cherish could talk people into things, but nothing she had said to Adam had helped. Maybe this really was the end for Bliss and Adam, as much as that was hard to believe.

As they drove along, listening to nothing but the clip-clopping of the horse's hooves, Bliss tried her best to put Adam Wengerd out of her mind. It seemed the more she tried not to think about him, though, the more she did think about him. At this point, she was sure she'd ruined her life. She and Adam would've had a good future and she was the one who'd messed it up. "You know something?"

"What?" Cherish asked.

"What hurts the most is I only have myself to blame. What hurts the second most is that there's not one single solitary thing I can do about it."

"That's not quite true," Cherish said.

Bliss looked over at her. "What can I do?"

"You can pray. Leave it in God's hands."

Bliss nodded. "I have been praying." It seemed a simple thing to say, but leaving something in God's hands and not worrying about it, that part was very hard.

"I've been praying too."

"Thank you." Bliss didn't say any more. There was such a hole in her heart without Adam. She didn't know how she'd ever get over it. "Cherish, just make sure you make the right decisions because some bad decisions can ruin your life. Just one bad one can."

"Okay. I'll do my best." Now Cherish knew she had to take her time getting to know someone before she rushed into a relationship. Adam had seemed so lovely. She never realized he could be so hard-hearted and unforgiving. "Have you been to the bishop?" Cherish asked.

"About Adam?"

"Yes. Maybe he could talk to him about forgiveness."

Bliss shook her head. "I don't want him back if he only forgives me because he's been told to. Thanks for thinking of that anyway. The other thing is, he might tell the bishop that I wrote to John. I'd feel awful if anyone else found out about that. It's embarrassing enough for both me and Debbie. I think I can trust Adam enough to keep quiet about it."

"Let me know if you think of anything I can do that might help."

"Thanks, Cherish, I will."

CHAPTER 23

The next day, Hope had planned to visit Christina with Debbie, but she'd come down with a cold so Debbie went alone while the girls and Wilma looked after Jared.

"Thanks for coming over," Christina said when she opened the door. "You'll have to bring Jared with you next time to see the babies."

"I will. They'll be good friends growing up."

"I know it."

"Do you have names yet? Ada made me promise I'd ask you."

"We do. Their names are Anna and Olivia. Anna is the oldest one."

"Nice names. I like them. Oh, and Ada wanted me to also ask if they have middle names, of course."

"No. I'm going to be like you and give my babies one name only. No middle names."

Debbie laughed. "Ada will be disappointed."

"I know. I got the speech about needing the middle

name, but the only people I have to please are myself and Mark."

"That's true. Can I tell everyone the names tonight? Ada, Samuel and Matthew will be there for the evening meal."

"Yes, I don't mind if you tell them. How are things going with you and Peter?"

"He's very supportive and I haven't had a lot of that in the past."

"How's he supportive?"

"He wants to be involved with Jared, and he's supportive of me making tea. He's doing everything he can to help."

"You need someone like that. Do you think you'll marry him?"

Debbie shrugged her shoulders. "I don't know. With everything that's happened to me, I've gone off the idea of marriage."

"Have you told Peter that?"

"No."

"But didn't you tell him not to move away when he had that job opportunity?"

"That was just to work with his uncle. I don't think it was a big opportunity."

"Aren't you wasting his time if you're not going to marry him?" asked Christina.

"No. He likes to spend time with me and we're getting to know each other. I told him how I felt."

"You did?"

"Yes. I'm pretty sure he knows how I feel. I told him I want to take things slow."

"That's good. Sorry. I didn't mean to pry. It's none of my business."

"I'm glad you asked. We're friends, almost family, so it's normal to ask."

When the babies woke, it was feeding time. Debbie helped Christina arrange pillows under the babies so she could feed them both at once.

While the babies were being fed, Debbie cleaned the kitchen and then swept and mopped the floors. By the time that was finished, Christina was yawning. Debbie changed the babies' diapers to give Christina a break and then the babies went down for another nap.

Debbie left Christina to have a rest while the babies were sleeping.

On the way home, Debbie thought about what Christina had said about Peter. Was she wasting his time?

She didn't have overwhelming feelings of love for him like she'd had for John, but just look how *that* had turned out. The only good thing to come from her marriage with John was Jared.

There was no one she could talk things over with right now. Wilma and Ada would just tell her that feelings for Peter would grow. Wilma's daughters didn't have enough experience with love. Hope and Joy had only ever loved one man and the younger daughters had never loved anyone, apart from Bliss. But she couldn't talk to Bliss about love—not after what happened with Adam.

Was she being selfish holding onto Peter? She hadn't thought much about stopping him from moving away until Christina had brought it up.

After dealing with her own parents and then John's

parents, it was almost too much to think about. Peter wasn't putting any pressure on her, so maybe he was happy with the way things were too. She hoped so because she enjoyed having someone look after her and make a fuss over her.

CHAPTER 24

*A*da, Samuel, and Matthew were at the Baker/Bruner household for the evening meal again. Debbie had held onto the information about the names until everyone was there. It had been difficult, as she was excited and couldn't wait to tell them.

"What have you decided to do, Matthew? Everyone's here and I think it's about time they knew," Ada said.

Matthew cleared his throat. "Okay, everyone. I've been working part time at the saddlery store for Mark as you all know. Fairfax has offered me a job at the orchard. Not your orchard, just his orchard."

"It's not his orchard," Ada corrected. "It belongs to Florence."

"I know that."

"Then why call it Fairfax's orchard just because his parents once owned it?"

"Yes, that's so, but it's the easiest way for everyone to know which orchard I'm talking about."

"We're not simpletons, Matthew," Wilma said with a laugh. "So you're staying on?"

"I am, if everyone doesn't mind." He looked round at everyone.

"We're all happy about that," Samuel said.

Favor agreed. "I'm glad."

"Good."

Wilma asked, "So you're staying permanently with Ada?"

"No. I've arranged to stay at Fairfax's old cottage. I'll be housemates with someone else. I haven't met him yet."

"An *Englisher?*" Levi asked.

"Yes, I think so. And don't worry there won't be parties and wild nights and drinking. This man is older and he's a quiet-living man, so Fairfax said."

"If it doesn't work out, you can always move back in with us," Ada told him.

"Thank you. I think it will be all right. I'll just be there to eat and sleep. I'm not there to become best buddies with my housemate."

"Not if he's an *Englisher,*" Wilma commented. "I'm surprised that Fairfax arranged such a thing."

"Don't fuss, *Mamm,*" Favor said. "It'll be okay. Just go with it and everything will work out."

Wilma rolled her eyes. "All the adults at the table are just trying to prevent you younger ones from making mistakes."

Cherish said, "I'm the youngest and that means we're all adults at the table. I think we should be free to make our own mistakes."

"Cherish has a point," Samuel said, earning a glare

from Ada.

"How do you figure that out?" Ada asked him.

Samuel put his fork down and finished his mouthful. "People learn from mistakes. It's not believable to expect no one makes any errors during their life. We're all human."

"That's true, Samuel, but errors are painful sometimes. We're trying to stop them from having to go through that pain," Wilma said, siding with Ada.

Debbie got up and excused herself and hurried out of the room. She was closely followed by Bliss.

"Is it something I said?" Wilma asked.

Favor picked up a chicken leg and munched on it. She chewed and swallowed before saying, "They both think they've made terrible mistakes. Hey, wait. Both their mistakes involved John." Favor laughed.

"Don't laugh at the misfortunes of others," Wilma told her.

"I'm not. I'm laughing at John."

"That's worse," Wilma said.

Cherish whispered to Favor, "He's dead."

"I'm not laughing because he's dead. I just realized that they're both upset about John. That's why I laughed. I wasn't really laughing at him. You people are so judgmental."

"Don't be rude, Favor. Bliss is upset about Adam. I don't think she's upset about John," Ada said.

Wilma set her knife and fork down. "Will we ever be able to just have a happy family dinner with everyone staying at the table? It seems someone is always running off."

Samuel said, "There do seem to be a lot of arguments here. More than what we had when our children were younger."

Ada smiled. "That's right. We had happy times around our table, didn't we, Samuel?"

He nodded.

Wilma pressed her lips together and then said, "That's because girls are harder to raise than boys."

"And how would you know that, Wilma, since you only had girls?"

Cherish held her breath and looked at her mother. Was Ada forgetting about Wilma's first born—the child Wilma's sister raised?

Mamm didn't seem to notice. "That's what you told me, Ada. You said your sons were easier than your daughters."

"Did I say that?" Ada asked.

"You did."

"Oh, well it must be true. I can't recall saying it, though."

"Cherish, why don't you run upstairs and check on Debbie and Bliss?" Levi suggested.

Cherish didn't want to. She had no idea what to say to either of them to make them feel better. "Maybe they both need someone older to talk with them."

Ada laughed. "You're an adult when it suits you, it seems."

Cherish nodded. "That's true and I think both of them could use your wisdom, Ada. The wisdom that's come from all your years of life experience."

"That's true. Never send a girl to do a woman's job.

Come on, Wilma. While the girls fix dessert, let's see if we can coax them downstairs to finish their meals."

Wilma and Ada left the table.

"Ada brought chocolate cake for dessert," Samuel announced.

"*Wunderbaar.* She's such a good cook," Matthew said.

Cherish finished off her chicken, thinking about nothing in particular.

"Are you pleased I'm staying on, Cherish?" Matthew opened his mouth and guided in his last forkful of chicken.

Cherish looked up, surprised he'd say such a thing in front of everyone. "Of course I am. Your three good deeds a day might come in handy when I need a favor."

Everyone laughed.

"I'm pleased too," said Favor. "It's someone else around here that's our age."

Matthew finished his mouthful. "Well, I am a little older than both of you."

"Are you?" Favor asked.

"I am. I'm just a late bloomer. I'll be well over six feet tall when I finish growing."

"How do you figure that?" Cherish asked. "Your brothers aren't even that tall, are they?"

"I'm not sure, but I'm taller than they were at my age. I figure... I just figured it out."

Favor's face scrunched. "When does someone finish growing?"

"Men can grow even after they're twenty," Matthew said.

"I didn't know."

"Now you do."

Cherish noticed Samuel and Levi exchange looks.

"There's nothing wrong with being short," Samuel told Matthew.

"Who's short?" Matthew asked.

"No one. I just said there's nothing wrong with it."

Matthew sat there looking a little upset. "I think we're ready for the cake now."

Cherish and Favor cleared the table of dishes and then placed the clean dessert bowls and plates on the table. Just as they were carrying the cake and the fruit salad to the table, Ada and Wilma came back into the room followed by Bliss and Debbie.

"Let's just everyone be happy," Wilma said. "Unwise things were said, Bliss and Debbie, and I'm sorry about that. Let's all move forward."

Ada said, "Debbie, you went to visit the twins today, didn't you?"

Debbie smiled, thinking about the babies. "I did."

"Well, have they come up with names?"

"Oh my, they're taking a long time about it," *Mamm* said.

"They have names now." Debbie got ready to address the issue about no middle names.

Wilma and Ada leaned forward and all eyes were on Debbie.

"Shall we try to guess?" Favor asked.

"No. Hush, Favor." *Mamm* glared at Favor.

Debbie took a deep breath. "Their names are Anna and Olivia."

Levi nodded. "Nice names."

"Delightful," Wilma agreed.

"I think so too. What about their middle names?" Ada asked.

Debbie shook her head. "They decided not to give them middle names."

Ada's eyes opened wide. "I'm not going to say anything about that. I already told Christina my thoughts on the matter."

Matthew kept eating and didn't say a word.

"What do you think, Matthew?" Samuel asked.

Matthew looked up. "About what?"

"About a middle name," Samuel said.

"Oh that. I'm not bothered."

Ada narrowed her eyes at Matthew. "You of all people should have an opinion on this."

"If they don't have a middle name then it's okay. At least they each have a name," Matthew said.

"And if they grow up and don't like their name, it's too bad. Is that right?" Ada asked. "Because they can't use their middle name like you did."

"Why does it bother you so much, Ada?" Levi asked.

"It's something that niggles me. It's not so much the name, but when I give my time to tell someone my opinion and they don't listen, it's annoying."

"Are you annoyed at me, Ada?" Debbie asked.

"I wasn't thinking about you just now, but you're right, you didn't listen to me either."

"But I did, and so did Christina. I thought about it and decided I didn't want to give Jared a middle name. Your comments made me think more about it."

"And that's her baby so it's her choice," Favor said.

Mamm glared at Favor. "You don't talk to adults like that. I've told you before. If you do that again, I won't take you to the farm with us."

"I'm Favor, *Mamm*, I'm not Cherish. Cherish is the one going to the farm."

"I know that, but I was thinking of taking you too. If you'll behave."

Favor jumped up and leaped into the air. "Really? I'd love to go somewhere—anywhere, even the farm. Do you mean it? Are you serious, Mamm?"

Mamm nodded. "If I see some decent behavior."

Favor looked over at Ada. "I'm sorry for what I said."

"I would hope so. I'm only trying to help. That's all I ever do."

"I know." Favor nodded. Then she clapped her hands before sitting back down. "I can't believe I get to go somewhere. This is so exciting."

"Can I take Caramel?" Cherish asked.

"No," *Mamm* said. "I think he'll be happier staying here. He'll take up too much room in the house."

"I'll look after him," Debbie said.

"So will I," said Samuel.

"I thought you didn't like dogs," Bliss said to Debbie.

Debbie giggled. "I know, but Caramel and I have been getting along. I'm starting to like him a little."

Cherish was pleased she had two volunteers to look after her dog. "Okay thanks. He needs a lot of attention."

"I'll look after Tommy and Timmy," Bliss said.

"Thanks, Bliss."

"We won't be gone that long. We're aiming to leave January second," Wilma said.

CHAPTER 25

*C*herish was delighted when she got a real letter from Simon, through the postal service. After she read it, she wanted someone's opinion. Her mother would only have negative things to say. Ada thought Simon was wonderful because she was friends with his parents. What she needed was to talk with someone who didn't know him. Then Cherish realized she needed to talk with Florence.

She made an excuse to leave the house and headed through the orchard to see her older half-sister.

Florence was enjoying her easier life. Fairfax, her newly appointed orchard manager was back, and it was also winter, so things were slow. That gave her time to recover from the hectic schedule. And, moving forward, things would be even better. The steel frame of the house was up and for the first time, Florence could see an end to the building work that had gone on for more than a year.

Carter had finally stopped making changes to the new house, thanks to the architect saying he was locking in the plans and the frame had gone up, so no further changes would be accepted.

Having become used to living in the small two bedroom cottage, Florence didn't know how she'd get used to living in a six bedroom three bathroom home. It seemed such a waste to have so many bedrooms since they didn't want a lot of children. Their ideal number was two since Florence felt she'd already raised her six younger half-sisters.

Florence heard a noise outside and thought it was Carter back from his meeting in town. When Spot jumped off the couch and started barking, she knew it wasn't him.

She looked outside and there was Cherish. Florence opened the door and saw her sister had an envelope in her hand.

"Hi, Florence. What are you doing?" At that moment, Carter's car pulled up alongside the house.

"I'm waiting for Carter to come home, and here he is."

"Oh, I brought you a letter from Simon. I just want you to tell me if you think he likes me."

"Come in. Do you mind if Carter sees it?"

Cherish shrugged. "I guess not. Two opinions are better than one."

Several minutes later, Cherish, Carter and Florence were sitting down with coffee while Iris sat on a cushion watching TV.

Cherish read out her letter from Simon. After that, she looked up at them. "Well, what do you think?"

Carter frowned. "I think it's strange that he wants his parents to go to the farm with him."

"He said they're like friends more than parents."

Carter laughed. "There's a red flag right there."

"Oh, Carter." Florence shook her head.

"What do you mean?" Cherish asked.

"I got along well with my folks too, but I wouldn't have taken them somewhere with me if I was interested in a girl. I wouldn't take my friends either. Sounds like he might be too attached to them, if you know what I mean."

"I don't think it's like that."

"Neither do I. Just ignore him," Florence said.

Carter leaned back on the couch. "Ignore me at your own peril."

Cherish laughed. "So are you going to give me a lecture about old people, knowing better?"

"What old people?" Carter asked.

"She means you," Florence told him.

Carter chuckled. "No, I'm not going to give you a lecture. You can find out for yourself. You might even like a man like that. They say when you marry someone you marry their family as well. You might as well get to know them too."

"Let's not get ahead of things. I'm not marrying anyone. I do like him. I'll admit to that."

"What's so special about him?" Florence asked.

"I don't know. There's just something about him."

"I think that's called chemistry."

"And all this mushy stuff is my cue to leave. I've got work waiting for me in the kitchen." Carter stood up.

When he walked out, Cherish asked Florence, "He's cooking?"

"Not tonight. His office is also the kitchen. We're so

cramped in this house. We're going to go from having too little space to having way too much."

Cherish wasn't really listening, she was too involved with thinking about Simon. "This is the first time I've met someone that I can see a future with. I mean, I have liked some men before but they haven't been very good for one reason or another."

"You don't have to rush in. Take your time."

"I am taking my time. I don't want to make a mistake like Debbie made. I don't mean to be rude, but John wasn't very nice. I'm also shocked by Adam's attitude toward Bliss so all these things are concerning."

"I heard about Adam and Bliss. I thought they would've been back together by now."

Cherish shook her head. "I don't think it's going to happen."

"I can't believe that. I think he'll come around."

"I hope so. Anyway, what do you think of my letter?"

Florence looked down at it. "It sounds hopeful. He really likes you too so that's great."

"Don't forget what I said," Carter called out from the kitchen.

Florence whispered to Cherish, "And that's another reason we need a bigger house."

Cherish giggled. She looked at Iris, who was sitting and watching the TV. "I can't get used to it. I'd probably watch it all day too if I could. If we had one, which we never will."

"Carter and I do like watching shows at night—documentaries, nature shows, and such. Sadly, watching the TV is all that Iris seems to want. She cries until we turn it on. We never should've allowed her to watch it to start with."

"What will you do about that?"

"We've been limiting her to just an hour. We're trying to distract her with other things, but it hasn't been easy to entertain her with the weather being so cold. She loves being outside, but the weather isn't being agreeable."

"What did we do when we were that young?"

"You and your sisters played with each other, or played with simple wooden toys. You just seemed to entertain yourselves."

Cherish looked down at the letter. "I'm glad you think he likes me."

"I'm sure he does, but it's what you think of him that counts. Don't like him just because he likes you."

"I won't."

"Do you want me to make you a new dress?" Florence offered.

"You mean it?"

"Yes."

"Oh, I'd love that."

"I've got a new electric machine. I still use the treadle sometimes. It'll only take me two days to finish it."

"I can't wait. What color would be good for me?"

"How about I get the fabric, choose the color and I'll surprise you with it."

Cherish wasn't so sure about that, but Florence seemed to be so excited that she didn't want to ruin the moment. "I'd love that. I haven't had a new dress for a while. All mine are hand-me-downs. We're leaving on the second. You know what colors I like, don't you?"

"I do." Florence sighed. "I can't help but be concerned about Bliss."

Cherish leaned closer. "Did you hear why they broke up?"

"Yes. Favor told me all about it."

Cherish gritted her teeth. "It figures. She can't keep her mouth shut. She's the one who told everyone. If it weren't for her, Bliss and Adam would still be together."

"She says it was your fault for finding the letters."

Cherish shrugged her shoulders. "I can't help that. I didn't know what I would find. I was just trying to discover why Bliss and Debbie didn't get along. And, I found out."

"That's for sure."

"At least Debbie and Bliss have cleared the air now, once Debbie got over the shock of the letters."

Florence nodded. "It would've been hard for her to hear."

"It was. Thanks for letting me share my letter with you."

"Anytime and don't listen to Carter. I think it's nice that Simon wants his parents to go with him."

"Good. I'll write back and tell him his folks are very welcome. I should get back home. I just needed a quick opinion on this." She got down on the floor and said goodbye to Iris. She managed to get a smile from her.

Carter stuck his head around the corner. "Remember what I said, Cherish. You don't want someone who lets his parents lead him around by the nose. You need a man who'll stand up for you."

"I'll remember. Bye, Carter."

After Carter said goodbye, Florence walked her to the door. Then she whispered, "Don't worry about what he said. He's being overly dramatic."

"I think so too. Simon is nothing like that. Maybe he thinks his parents need a break from their farm."

"What?" Carter yelled out. "They need a break from their farm to go to another farm?"

Cherish's mouth fell open. "The sound sure does travel in this place. You do need a bigger house."

Florence laughed and then she hugged Cherish goodbye.

Cherish walked back through the orchard, concerned about what Carter had said. Then she dismissed it, reasoning that Carter was an *Englisher*. Besides, Florence agreed with her.

CHAPTER 26

*W*hen Cherish's house came into view, she was delighted to see Joy's horse and buggy by the barn. She picked up her pace, hurrying toward the house.

After she greeted Joy and Faith, Joy's daughter, *Mamm* had Cherish start peeling the vegetables for dinner. Cherish sat and peeled at one end of the table, while everyone gathered around the other end.

Joy said, "Isaac and I are looking forward to Christmas. Will Christina and Mark be coming here for the Christmas family dinner too?"

Mamm answered, "I haven't asked them yet, but I hope so. I'd love to have the new twins here to celebrate with us for our Christmas dinner."

"Christina won't be leaving the house until they're a lot older," Cherish said. "It's a lot harder with twins."

Ada suggested, "Wilma, we should get the ladies together and visit Christina once a week. Since she can't go out, we'll come to her."

"Does that include me?" Joy asked.

"Of course it does."

"I like that idea, Ada. We'll get it organized immediately. I think Christina will appreciate it."

"I think she will too," Wilma said.

Joy raised her eyebrows. "It's a shame no one thought of that when I had Faith. I was often so lonely."

"But you were going out a couple of days after you gave birth," *Mamm* said.

"I wouldn't have had to if anyone offered to visit. No one visited me for months."

"I don't think that's true, Joy. We all visited you."

"Early on you did, but now I hardly see anyone. Anyway, what does that matter now? That was a long time ago. It's a great idea for Christina."

"Yeah, sounds like loads of fun," Cherish said.

Everyone stared at Cherish. "We don't need your sarcasm," Ada said. "It might not seem much to you, but you're spoiled. You've never been by yourself because you've always had people around you."

"I never asked for it. I can't help it."

Joy appeared to agree with Ada. "Just try to be a little more understanding of people, Cherish. It's very isolating for me when Isaac goes to work and I'm home alone all day with Faith. I can't talk with her. She's too young, so it's not the same as having an adult around."

"Sorry I said anything."

"Make us some tea, would you?" Ada asked. "And you know I like mine extra hot."

"So, do I peel the vegetables or make the tea?" Cherish asked.

"Make the tea," Ada told her. "Then you can go back to the vegetables."

Joy continued talking, "I'd love people to visit me more. I can't really get out unless I wake up super early and wake Faith too and take Isaac to work so I can have the buggy for the day."

Cherish got up to make the tea. "You sure complain a lot, Joy." Cherish hadn't meant to voice her thought. It just slipped out of her mouth.

Mamm pressed her lips together, then she said, "It's not complaining when she's just saying how she feels."

"Okay. Sorry, Joy. I didn't mean to say something wrong."

Joy looked at her mother and then Ada. "Does everyone else think I complain a lot?"

"Of course we don't." Ada patted Joy's hand. "Don't listen to Cherish. She's too young to know what she's talking about."

"I might be young, but that doesn't mean I'm unaware of things. I'm young and smart," Cherish said.

Mamm laughed. "I don't know about that. Young and loud might be more fitting."

Cherish filled up the teakettle.

"I can't believe you're taking her back to the farm, *Mamm*. You said yourself she doesn't even need to go," Joy whined. "I'll even feel more alone with you gone."

Cherish lit the gas flame and placed the teakettle on top, hoping her mother would tell Joy that she did need to go back to the farm.

"I've said I'll take her. That was before I knew about that young man that's coming there too."

"Who's that?" Joy asked.

Ada answered, "He's a delightful young man, Simon. He's a good family friend. Samuel and I have known his family for years. We just found out he doesn't live far from Cherish's farm. He's going to visit her when she's there."

"So you're helping her find a man before Favor? And what about Bliss?" Joy asked. "Surely Bliss needs more attention."

"No, Joy, you're wrong. It's nothing like that. Simon just happens to live close. I met him at Hope's wedding and after that I found out who he was and where he lives. There's nothing in it," Cherish said. "We're not dating. That's just ridiculous. He's just a friend."

"I know it is. You're far too young in the head to get married. Some say that I married young, but I think I was mature for my age." Joy looked over at Favor and Bliss who had just walked into the kitchen.

"We were just talking about you, Bliss. Come sit beside me," Ada said.

"How have you been, Bliss?" Joy asked.

"Fine."

Joy said, "I think you need to find a nice man so you can stop being upset about Adam."

"You shouldn't remind her of him," Favor told Joy.

"It's okay. Everything reminds me of Adam." Bliss let out a loud sigh.

Matthew walked into the kitchen and looked around. "Why's everyone so quiet? Were you all talking about me? Is that why you stopped talking just now?"

Ada laughed and everyone else smiled. "No. We're just

having our usual disagreements over one thing or another."

Matthew looked at Cherish. "Ah, making coffee, are you?"

"I can make you a cup. Why aren't you at the saddlery store?"

"I've finished for the day. Mark is working the last two hours."

"I do worry about Christina by herself with the twins," Ada said.

"Don't worry. She's not by herself. Mark said Krystal was there, helping her this afternoon."

"Krystal?" Favor asked.

"Yes."

"She didn't tell me she was helping Christina. She's supposed to be working in the quilt store," Favor said.

"I don't know where she's supposed to be, but right now she's with Christina. That's what Mark said and he'd know."

Ada clasped her hands and set them on the table. "I'm glad the girl is making herself useful. Yes, she made mistakes with the lying and whatnot, but she's turned a corner as far as I'm concerned. Gertie is happy with her and she's a hard woman to please."

Cherish knew there was only one reason that Krystal was helping anyone. She wanted all the single men to think she was a good Christian woman, who worked tirelessly to help others. It couldn't be further from the truth as Cherish perceived it. Krystal was working tirelessly to help one person and one person alone. That person was Krystal.

CHAPTER 27

Three days after Florence had agreed to make her a dress, Cherish went back to check on the progress. She took Bliss with her to get her out of the house and keep her mind occupied.

With Bliss on one side and Caramel on her other side, Cherish nearly skipped through the orchard. "I haven't had a new dress in years. A good one, I mean. Florence is an excellent seamstress. When she was still living at home, she used to make all the clothes for the family. We still wear many of those dresses."

"Sounds like they were made to last, handed from older sister to the younger sisters."

"You've got that right. Sadly, I was the youngest and many of the clothes got all worn out by the time they came down to me."

"I never had that problem with two older brothers."

"That's right, you're the only girl."

"I was until I joined your family."

"I hope I look good in the new dress. Simon might appreciate me looking pretty."

They walked through the orchard and then she slipped through the fence that divided the two properties, helped Bliss get through without her clothes catching, and they walked up to the door and knocked on it.

Carter answered the door and stared at Cherish. "You're back, and you've brought Bliss."

"I sure am back. I believe Florence has been sewing a dress for me."

"Yes I think so."

Iris came running toward her, reaching her chubby arms towards her. Cherish leaned down and scooped the little girl into her arms. "Good morning, Iris. Can you say Aunt Cherish? Aunt Cherish is my favorite?"

"Hey unfair," Bliss said. "What about me?"

Carter laughed. "I'll just get her for you. She's upstairs."

"Cherish is my favorite. Say it."

Iris made an attempt at saying it.

"Pretty good. We can work on it."

"Come to me," Bliss said, clapping her hands.

Iris looked over and reached out her hands to Bliss.

"Oh, you're leaving me," Cherish said, "You're my favorite too, but don't tell anybody."

Florence came downstairs and Cherish looked up to see a dark pinkish-red, almost magenta, dress in her half-sister's hands.

"Wow. It's bright," Bliss blurted out.

"Oh no, I was worried about that. Is it too bright?" Florence asked.

"No. I think I'll be able to get away with it," Cherish said.

Iris struggled, so Bliss put her on the floor just as Florence handed the dress to Cherish.

"Do you want to try it on?"

Cherish held it against herself. "I think this looks about right." Then Cherish had a closer look at the dress. "I wish I was as good at sewing as this."

"You could be. All you need to do is practice. I've shown you how to sew many a time."

"I know that."

"All you have to do is put your mind to something and practice it. If you keep doing it over and over again, you'll get good at it," Bliss said.

"That's right. That's all I did," Florence agreed.

"Yes, but I don't like putting effort into anything."

Florence laughed. "Are you serious?"

"Kind of."

"What you need to do is find something that you enjoy doing and then you'll be happy to put the effort into it until you become good at it."

Cherish shrugged her shoulders. "I know, that's what everybody says."

"Really? I don't like to be the same as everybody else. Who says that?"

"Mostly Ada, I think."

"Are you sure you don't want to try it on, Cherish?" Bliss asked.

"No, that's okay. I'll put it on when I get home. I'm sure it will fit."

"I think it will too. Are you sure the color's all right? I can make you another one before you go to the farm."

"It's perfect."

"I thought it suited your personality. When I saw it in the fabric store, I couldn't resist it."

Cherish leaned forward and gave her a hug. "It's simply perfect."

"Good. I hope it does the job."

"What job?" Bliss asked.

"You know, what we were talking about on the way here."

"Oh that." Bliss giggled. "I hope it does the job too, then."

Cherish gave a nervous laugh. "We'll see. Anyway, it doesn't hurt to have another friend, does it? Simon will be a good friend at the very least."

"Yes, at your age, that's all you need to be worried about. There will be plenty of time for boyfriends." Florence smiled at her, raising her eyebrows. It was something *Mamm* did when she was trying to assure her of something. It was the first time Florence had reminded her of *Mamm*.

Cherish nodded. "That's what everyone says. *Mamm* says it the most."

"Oh no, again? Seems I'm becoming boring and predictable."

Cherish stared at her, not knowing what to say. Florence had always been boring and predictable, as far back as she could remember. "That's what comes from being the older sister," she said.

"Yes well, I suppose it does. When are you leaving?" Florence asked.

"Not until after Christmas. On the second of January, *Mamm* says. Unless she can't get a car for that day."

"That's right. You told me the date when you were here the other day. Have a good time there."

"I always do."

"Say hello to Malachi for me," Florence said.

Cherish rolled her eyes.

"Why did you do that?" Bliss asked.

Cherish shrugged her shoulders. "I forgot about Malachi."

Florence folded her arms. "How could you forget about your farm manager?"

"I've been too busy thinking about Simon, I guess. Oh and then I'll probably have to put up with Annie Whiley as well."

"Don't you get along with her?" Florence asked.

"She's okay I guess. But Malachi and she are way too friendly. I think they're dating, but he denies it. I still think they are."

Florence laughed. "Did you ask him?"

"Of course I did. Like I said, he denied it. Thanks for the dress. Now I'll have to go somewhere nice while I'm at the farm so I get a chance to wear it."

"What about the Sunday meeting while you're away?" Bliss suggested.

"I will wear it if we're going to be there for it. *Mamm* doesn't want to go for a whole week, so we might miss out. They have fortnightly meetings there, same as here."

Florence looked at Bliss. "I'm sorry to hear about you and Adam."

"Thanks. It's okay. I'm getting used to it now."

"You don't think there's—"

"No chance at all. We should go, Cherish."

"Yes, we should. We've got a lot to do. Thanks again, Florence. I love the dress. It's amazing."

"You're welcome."

Carter came out from the kitchen. "Do come and tell us all about your trip when you get back."

"I will."

CHAPTER 28

*W*ith her dress over her arm, Cherish walked into the utility room to get a hanger.

Mamm looked up from the kitchen table where she was drinking tea with Ada. "What's that you've got there, Cherish?"

"A new dress. Florence made it for me to wear if we go anywhere special while we're at the farm."

"We've got Christmas to get through first." Wilma stared at Cherish. "Why did you want a new dress?"

"She offered to make me one."

Wilma pursed her lips. "As a Christmas gift?"

Cherish slipped the dress onto the hanger. "I'm not sure. She didn't say so. She just asked if I wanted her to make me one, and I said yes. I haven't had anything new for so long."

"No point in you having anything new when your sisters' old clothes fit you just as well."

"By the time they come down to me, they're all worn out."

SAMANTHA PRICE

"I know that happens sometimes, that's why you've had new clothes in the past. We just can't give you new things all the time," *Mamm* said.

"I understand that, *Mamm,* and I'm not complaining."

Ada's lips turned down at the corners. "You're certainly doing a lot of talking about it though."

"Mamm started it so I was just explaining what happened. Should I be silent next time?"

"Ah, silence. What I'd give for a whole day of silence. That would be golden." Ada put her teacup up to her lips and took a sip.

Cherish was tempted to tell her to go home if she wanted silence, but she was too scared of Ada to say that.

"We'll never have silence, Ada. I'm fine with that. I'm determined to enjoy as much of Favor and Cherish as I can before they leave us," *Mamm* said.

Ada huffed. "You can't keep them here."

Cherish said, "I will be moving to the farm. You'll have to get used to the idea of that, *Mamm."*

"When?" Ada asked.

"In a year. I'll be way over eighteen by then."

Mamm frowned. "Way over? Hardly. Only by a few months."

"Still. You can enjoy me for a year, *Mamm."* Cherish put the dress on the table and sat down with them.

"You might change your mind. What is there at the farm for you? Just keep Malachi there and he can run the farm for you," *Mamm* suggested.

"Nee. That ruins the whole point of having the farm."

"Let her try it out, Wilma. She'll be home in no time once she realizes how hard it is."

"No I won't. I know what it's like there—I lived there, remember? Helping Aunt Dagmar with all of the work. I know I might get lonely, but Favor or Bliss might want to move there."

"I don't think so. Bliss will be back with Adam before long. I just know it," Ada said. "And I don't think Favor will leave this community or her family and her friends to live at your farm."

Cherish shrugged. "I'll go by myself then."

"I think you'll have to. And then I think you won't be there for long before you decide to come back."

"It's not that isolated. Simon doesn't live that far."

"Too far to go there and back in one day."

"He can stay overnight. He's bringing his parents. I got a letter from him and he said when he visits, he's bringing them. So they'll be staying at the farm too."

"I'll be pleased to meet them. And there are enough bedrooms in the house, aren't there, Cherish?" Ada asked.

"There are five bedrooms. One for Malachi, one for Simon, one for Simon's parents, Favor and I can share, and that still leaves one for you, *Mamm.*"

Ada counted them up on her fingers. "That's five."

"I know."

"How long will they be staying?" *Mamm* asked.

"I'm not sure. I didn't ask. It doesn't matter, does it?"

"No. We'll take enough supplies from here to feed everyone."

Cherish shrugged. "Okay, if you want, but there will be enough food on the farm."

"Still, I like to be sure. I can't have anyone going hungry."

"It is lovely and peaceful on your farm, Cherish. I have enjoyed my visits there," Ada said.

"Good."

Ada stared at the dress. "That's very bright."

"But not too bright, is it?"

Ada smiled. "I like it. What do you say, Wilma?"

"Well, since Cherish didn't ask my opinion, it hardly matters."

Cherish had to ask, "What do you think, *Mamm?*"

"I like it. It's a happy color, for a girl who's becoming a lady, but not too quickly." *Mamm* stared at Cherish, as though she was trying to make a point.

"What will Malachi do when you move back there?" Ada asked, still talking about the farm.

"I'm not sure. We haven't discussed it. He knows I'm coming back. Perhaps this time, I'll tell him exactly when I'm coming back so he can start making plans."

"Good idea," Ada said. "Just don't leave yourself without a manager."

Cherish had it all figured out. "It won't matter. If he leaves earlier, I'll have to move there. I'm old enough to move there now, but I'm staying on here for you, *Mamm.*"

"Aren't you lucky, Wilma?" Ada said. "*Gott* is blessing you with your loving daughter for an extra year.

"I know." Wilma laughed as she got up and topped up the water in the teakettle. Then she lit the stove and placed the kettle on top.

"Will you take your birds with you, Cherish?" Ada asked just as *Mamm* sat down with them.

"Of course I will. I'll be taking everything with me. Timmy, Tommy, and Caramel."

168

Ada grunted. "It'll certainly be quiet without you. That's all I'm saying on the matter. But, as I said before, you might go there and find you don't like it and then you'll move back here. Then the best thing you could do is sell the farm."

Cherish sat there looking at Ada. "I'm never selling the farm. It was Aunt Dagmar's."

"Yes, but she wouldn't expect you to have a tough life away from your family. She'd be happy if you're happy."

"And I will be happy at the farm. I've always said I'm moving there. I think that everybody has to get used to that idea." There was a silent moment where Cherish stared at each woman in turn. She had thought they'd get used to the idea by now. She'd been telling them what she was going to do for the past few years.

Ada took a deep breath. "We hear you, but the reality of it all will be very different from the story you're telling yourself about it. Yes you were there with Dagmar, but I'm sure you didn't see everything she was doing every day. It'll take a lot of hard work. And like I said before, there are always house repairs and barn repairs."

"I'm figuring that out. It can't be that hard. It's just a matter of learning what to do." Cherish offered a bright smile to show them that they weren't discouraging her in the slightest.

"Don't bother, Ada. She's someone who can't be told anything. She'll have to find out for herself."

"That's right. I'll find out for myself, so what's all the fuss?" Cherish asked.

Ada shrugged her shoulders. "I'm just trying to save you some pain."

"Thanks for the thought."

The kettle whistled. "Who's making the tea?" Ada asked. "I need another cup before Wilma and I start sewing the quilt. This one has gone cold. Cherish, you can make the tea because you made me talk so much that I neglected to drink this cup."

"I'll get it." Cherish got up and turned toward the pot that had just boiled. She took the kettle off the stove and poured the water into the teapot.

"Did you put tea leaves in the pot?" Wilma asked.

"No. I didn't. You were talking too much."

"So it's my fault?" Wilma complained.

"Kind of."

"Why don't we try some of Debbie's tea, Wilma?"

"That's right. I must have been thinking you might want to try some of Debbie's tea and that's why I didn't put your usual tea leaves in right away."

Ada and Wilma laughed at her, and she soon joined in.

Cherish picked up a jar from Debbie's selection of teas. "The lemon tea was the most popular when we did the tasting."

"Have we tried the lemon, Wilma?"

"No. I haven't, anyway."

"Lemon it is then." Cherish shook in some tea leaves.

"Use a spoon," Ada ordered.

"Too late. Now, I'll let that sit for a while."

Ada shook her head. "You know I like it hot."

"It'll be hot." Cherish went to the shelf for a clean towel and wrapped it tightly around the teapot.

"I hope so. That's a good idea—wrapping it up, I mean."

CHAPTER 29

*A*fter she made Ada and Wilma another pot of tea, Cherish took her new dress upstairs to her bedroom. While she was hanging it up, Favor walked in the door.

"Was this your idea about me going to the farm, Cherish?" She sat on the bed.

"No, because I didn't think *Mamm* would let you. You know how she's always going on about us doing work and all that."

"I know. We'll have such fun."

"I know it. I'm so excited. I'm glad you're coming." Cherish was in such a good mood, almost nothing could ruin it.

"You're always talking about the farm and I've never seen it. I might even move there with you when I'm older."

"I'd love that. You can tell me what you think about Malachi. I guess you'll meet Annie Whiley too. She'll probably be hanging around talking about her gingerbread houses. Oh, I shouldn't be mean. She really is a nice girl. I'll make more of an effort to get to know her this time."

"I already met Annie at Hope's wedding."

Cherish sat on the bed next to Favor. "Oh that's right. It's weird that she was there at the wedding, don't you think?"

"Not really."

"I thought it was odd. She only knew me and Samuel and Ada. It was just an excuse to get Malachi to go somewhere with her, but it backfired because he didn't show up at all."

"He couldn't, could he? Who would've looked after the farm?"

"I don't know. One of his friends perhaps. He could've arranged something just for a few days."

"Why do you keep talking about Malachi when you like Simon?"

Cherish lifted her chin. "I do like Simon. I don't like Malachi at all. I don't know why you said that."

"Then what does my opinion on him matter?"

"It doesn't."

Favor sniggered. "Yeah right."

"Don't be annoying like that or I'll tell *Mamm* not to take you to the farm."

"Too late. She already said I could go. I wonder if she'll let Krystal go too. There would be enough room in the car."

"No. I don't want Krystal to go because you'll spend all your time with her and leave me out of everything."

"We wouldn't do that."

"Yes you would. You've done that ever since Krystal arrived."

"I suppose she has to stay here and work in the quilt store anyway. All right. We'll have fun together like we used to."

"That's right. She does." Cherish pointed to her dress. "What do you think about that?"

Favor stared at the dress. "It's beautiful. How did you get that?"

"Florence made it for me."

Favor's mouth fell open. "Where's mine?"

"Is she making you one too?"

"I don't know. If she made you one she should make me one."

"She offered to make it because she knew I was going to the farm and I'd see Simon."

"Unfair." Favor pouted. "I'm going to the farm too. I might meet some nice man."

"She would've made you one if she had known. I'm sure…"

"It doesn't matter, I'll just borrow yours."

"No you won't! That's my special dress. It's my new Sunday best."

"Such a pretty color. I want one just like that."

"I'd love that and then we'd be matching. Ask Florence to make you one when we get back."

"I sure will."

CHAPTER 30

*A*t daybreak on Christmas morning, Wilma sat by herself watching the winter sun rise over the tops of the apple trees. Over her first cup of coffee for the day, she pondered the events of the past year.

So much had happened.

Debbie had come to live with them and they had the added surprise of baby Jared, being a product of a secret marriage. That had been a tumultuous ride for poor Debbie, having to keep quiet about the marriage to her late husband so she wouldn't offend his parents.

Then there was the pleasant addition of Fairfax to their family after marrying Hope. A big surprise and a double blessing was Mark and Christina's twins.

There was also the *wunderbaar* news that Earl and Miriam would be parents of twins at some stage next year. Wilma smiled as she looked forward to the day she'd meet Earl's twins. She felt bad about cautioning both Earl and Miriam that Miriam would be too old to have babies.

Miriam had proved her wrong and, for once, Wilma was pleased to be wrong.

The year had brought some disappointment though, with Adam Wengerd turning away from Bliss. Hopefully, they'd reconcile soon and their rocky time would just be like a pothole in the journey of their relationship.

For now, Wilma was determined to enjoy the remaining girls left at home. She wasn't in a hurry for them to marry. The house would be way too quiet once they were all gone. She feared being left alone, and with Levi's heart problems, she knew being alone in the future was a real possibility for her.

When Wilma heard noises coming from upstairs, her mind started ticking over about traveling to Cherish's farm. She had to know how serious Cherish was about Simon. If he wasn't right for her, she wanted to be there to prevent Cherish from making an impulsive decision. That was the real reason she agreed to go to the farm this time. That and, she'd have extra time to spend with both Cherish and Favor. It would be a good time for her to reconnect with her youngest daughters.

Wilma poured herself a second coffee and stayed by the stove to warm herself. It had been a mild winter so far and she hoped the weather would remain that way for their drive to the farm. There was nothing worse than traveling in a blizzard.

Today, Christina had promised they would come with the twins, and Florence and Carter and Iris had been invited too, although Wilma wasn't sure that either couple would come. Anything with the twins might prevent Christina and Mark coming at the last minute. Florence and Carter's invitation had been late-notice. They'd never come to any other Christmas dinners, so Wilma held out little hope they'd come today.

An hour later, the girls were awake and in the kitchen helping to prepare the food. This year as well as the traditional turkey, she had decided on roasted chicken, stuffing, mashed potatoes and gravy, salads and a wide variety of desserts for the menu. Ada was cooking a pork roast with apple sauerkraut, and she was also bringing a couple of her specialty desserts. Hope was bringing salads and Joy was bringing her special apple custard dessert that everyone loved.

ADA, Matthew and Samuel arrived well before one in the afternoon, which was when the special meal was scheduled. Ada burst into the kitchen followed by Samuel and Matthew. "Whoopie pies and chocolate chip cookies. Put the boxes on the counter," Ada told the men. Then she greeted Wilma with a kiss. "I tried to do a gingerbread house but it fell flat again. I can't work out what I'm doing wrong. I need another lesson from Annie and her mother. Looks like I'll have to take you to the farm sometime next year, Cherish, so I can do just that."

"That would be great."

Favor whined, "She's already getting to go there in a few days. If you take her, that'll be twice in one year. Will I be able to go with her?"

"We'll see," *Mamm* said.

Bliss told Favor, "Just be pleased you're going this time."

Favor pouted at her, but Bliss kept setting the table without noticing.

Closer to one o'clock, Christina arrived bringing two store-bought cakes. Wilma was delighted to share Christmas with her stepson and his wife, and especially with their newborn twins.

Hope and Fairfax arrived at almost the same time, along with Joy, Isaac, and Faith. Their food offerings were brought into the kitchen amidst a flurry of greetings and hugs and hanging of coats.

Just before the meal was due to start, Wilma stepped out of the house and looked up the road. There was no sign of Florence and Florence was never late. That meant she wasn't coming.

Cherish stuck her head outside. "They only said they might come, *Mamm.*"

"I know."

"Carter said they're not that big on Christmas."

Wilma nodded. "I understand." Wilma headed back to the kitchen, thinking about her two eldest daughters, who lived too far away to come to family events.

Debbie sensed what was going on and put her arm around Wilma. "Just be happy with who is here rather than who isn't."

Tears filled Wilma's eyes. "Thank you, Debbie. You're right. I'm happy to share this day with everyone here."

Ada sighed as she looked at the table. "A gingerbread house would've made a delightful decoration for the center. Perhaps next year."

Cherish grinned. "There's always next year."

"Next year," Timmy said.

"Oh, did you hear that, everyone? Who heard that? Timmy clearly said next year." Cherish ran over to Timmy. "Oh, good boy, Timmy. Who's a pretty boy?"

Ada laughed. "I did hear something similar but it wasn't that clear."

"I heard it," Debbie said. "I thought it was clear."

Once Christina had fed the twins and they were both asleep, Wilma then called everyone to the table. "I hope everyone's hungry."

"We sure are," Matthew rubbed his tummy. "I've been saving up. I didn't eat breakfast."

Once seated, Mark looked over at Faith who sat by herself at a small children's table. "Next year, we'll have a few more children sitting at that table."

Ada gasped. "Oh, Christina, you're not having another baby, are you?"

Mark laughed and answered for her, "No. I meant our two might be sitting there. They should be sitting up by then."

"Give us a chance, Ada." Christina laughed.

When everyone settled, they closed their eyes and said their silent prayer of thanks.

AFTER EVERYONE HAD their fill of the main course and the desserts, Levi announced,

"Ladies, I'd have to say this is the best meal I've ever tasted. Thank you. And, the company's not been bad either."

"I agree," said Samuel.

"Me too," added Matthew, patting his tummy.

"Thanks for inviting us," Mark said.

"You're always welcome. You don't have to be invited, just show up," Wilma told him.

"For once, I feel this family cares about me. I know you all did before the twins came, but I had... I was too upset in my own grief to open my eyes to what was really going on," Christina said. "I don't know how Mark and I would've coped with the twins without the help and support from everyone at this table. I know other women have babies and can do all kinds of things and get back to normal fast, but it's taken me a long time."

"That's what happens with twins," Ada said. "It's not as easy as one. We've moved passed all our disagreements now, Christina. We're heading into a new year with new possibilities."

"Agreed," Wilma said. "We're grateful for both of you and the twins."

Mark smiled. *"Denke,* Wilma. I can't believe we have two babies. I'm still getting used to the idea I'm a *vadder* to two girls."

"The Lord has blessed each one of us," Samuel said.

"He has," Levi agreed.

While they all sat there, too full to move away from the table, Matthew had a suggestion.

"I know a game we could all play."

"What kind of game is that?" Ada asked.

"We will each be given a name of somebody sitting at this table. And without saying who we are, we have to talk and act like that person and then everybody else has to guess. The first person to guess gets a point. The person with the most points is the winner."

"That'll be easy," said Hope. "What's the prize?"

"Um, I hadn't thought of a prize. I don't have one."

"I might have an extra box of candies hidden away somewhere," Ada said.

"Excellent!" Samuel grinned. "The winner can have a box of candy."

Favor clapped her hands loudly until Cherish poked her side to make her stop.

"Okay. I'll need a piece of paper and a pen," Matthew said.

Wilma had Cherish fetch the paper and a pencil from the kitchen drawer.

Matthew wrote everybody's names down and then ripped the paper into sections. He mixed up the pieces in a bowl and took it around to everybody so they could select a name.

"When you get the name, don't show anyone." He sat back down.

"Who'll start first?" asked Wilma.

"Why don't you go first, Wilma?" Matthew said.

"Okay. What do I do? Can I stand up and walk around?"

"Yes, you can do whatever you want," Matthew told her. "Just act like the person whose name's on the bit of paper."

Wilma stood, pulled her shoulders back and lifted up her chin. "What are we going to do today? I am so bored.

Nothing ever happens around here. *Mamm,* stop being mean to Timmy and Tommy."

Everyone yelled out, "Cherish."

Wilma smiled and showed everyone the paper that said Cherish.

Matthew laughed. "Good guess. I think Favor was the first one to say Cherish's name. One point to Favor." He wrote that down on his notepad.

Favor clapped her hands. "Yes, I was first."

"Do you think I really act like that, *Mamm?*" Cherish pouted.

Ada leaned forward. "It's not only your mother who thinks that. Everyone else does too."

"Okay who's next? It's you, Samuel."

Samuel looked at his bit of paper. Then he stood up, adjusted his imaginary prayer *kapp,* frowned at everyone, and then gave an exaggerated giggle and clapped his hands loudly.

"Favor," Cherish shouted out.

"Ow, my ear, Cherish," Favor complained.

Cherish loved this game. Now she had one point and Favor had one. "I got that first. Write a point down for me, Matthew."

"This is fun," said Hope.

"How did you know about this game?" Ada asked Matthew.

"We played it a couple of times at home."

Then it was Cherish's turn. She had Ada. She got up off the chair and walked to the door. Then she walked towards the table with her shoulders hunched. Speaking in a crotchety voice, she said, "Wilma, why aren't the girls doing any work? You're not hard enough on them. Cherish, make me a cup of tea and make sure it's hot. You know I like it hot."

Everyone laughed and Samuel was the first to say it was Ada, earning a glare from his wife. She was the only one who didn't think it was funny.

"I don't talk like that, Cherish, and I certainly don't walk like that. I'm short so I make sure I stand tall."

Cherish delighted in saying, "Everyone guessed you, so…"

Ada scoffed. "That's ridiculous."

Matthew looked at Favor. "Your turn."

Favor let out a big yawn and covered her mouth and then said in a deep voice, "No, Bliss, you can't work at the café. I don't care that Cherish works there. Where's my paper? Has anyone seen it?"

"Levi!" everyone shouted before they chuckled.

Matthew scratched his head. "That's a hard one. I can't tell who was first."

"I think Hope was first with that one," *Mamm* said.

"Okay, Hope it is."

"I was before Hope," said Favor.

Hope shook her head. "I was the first."

"It should've been you, Bliss," Cherish said. "You should've guessed that one."

Bliss nodded, and her lips turned upwards at the corners. Although she was smiling, she wasn't happy. Adam loved Christmas and he hadn't come to see her. She'd spent most of the day looking out the window, in the hope that he'd at least come there to say hello.

Bliss thought back to the last Christmas dinner she'd

183

shared with Adam. They'd had such fun... but things were different now. It was hard to be happy and join in the fellowship and the laughter when her heart was broken into tiny pieces.

She looked at how happy Hope and Fairfax were. Then she saw Joy and Isaac with their young daughter, and Christina and Mark with their twins. Why had her happiness escaped from her?

Adam should've been there with her.

What plan did God have for her life that didn't include Adam? Bliss tried not to be bitter but she couldn't understand what God was doing.

When Jared cried upstairs, Bliss saw her chance to escape the fake smiles she'd been offering all day. "I'll check on him, Debbie."

"Would you? He's been fed. He might need his diaper changed. Then he should go back to sleep. He always sleeps longer than this."

"Okay."

"Are you sure?" Debbie asked.

"Quite sure. You stay." Bliss headed out of the room. As she headed up the stairs, the laughter got farther and farther away. She didn't belong with happy people. She felt better when she was alone. If Adam had any thoughts in the back of his head about reconciliation, he would've come to say hello, today of all days.

AT THE END of the guessing game, it was Favor who won the box of candies. She squealed with delight as Ada handed the box over. Then she opened it and shared it with everyone, but not everyone had any room left after the huge meal and the sumptuous desserts.

It was late afternoon when Christina and Mark left, followed quickly by Isaac and Joy.

The men were too full to move, so they stayed in the kitchen while everyone else cleaned up around them. After that, Favor and Cherish headed upstairs to share some candies with Bliss. Everyone knew she was still upset over Adam and the girls were determined to take her mind off him.

CHAPTER 31

Christmas had come and gone and the New Year arrived quietly. Today, Cherish, Wilma and Favor were leaving for the farm. Samuel, Ada and Matthew had come to the house early to say goodbye.

Cherish was already packed and was upstairs making her bed. Everyone else was gathered around the fire in the living room, waiting for the car to arrive.

"We'll miss you, *Mamm*, but don't worry, everything will be fine. We're taking more meals to Christina and we'll look after *Dat*," Bliss said.

"I'm not worried. I know you'll handle everything."

Favor said, "Thanks for letting me go too, *Mamm*."

"Well, you haven't been anywhere for a while. None of us have been anywhere since Earl and Miriam's wedding."

"You've been up north to see Honor and Mercy, Wilma. Did you forget that?" Ada asked.

"I meant, I've been away, but the girls haven't."

Cherish was even more excited when she looked out her window and saw the car. The day had finally arrived

187

and now the car was here, so for sure her mother wouldn't change her mind about going.

"Cherish, the car's here," Favor called out.

"I'm coming." Cherish hugged Caramel, who was asleep on her bed. "You be a good boy. Debbie is going to look after you and so will Bliss. And just between you and me, I've got Samuel checking up on them because he did such a good job of looking after you when I went to Earl and Miriam's wedding. I'll miss you."

He opened his eyes and gave her a lick up the side of her chin.

"Yuck." She wiped her cheek with the back of her hand.

"Cherish, we're paying the driver by the hour. Hurry up!" *Mamm* yelled out.

"Coming." Cherish grabbed her suitcase and headed out of the room. Debbie was at the bottom of the stairs, holding the baby. Cherish looked down at Jared. "Don't grow too fast while I'm gone."

Debbie laughed. "You'll be gone for less than a week."

"Unless I can talk *Mamm* into staying longer."

"Bye, Cherish. Have a good time."

"I will. Oh, you see your tea man today, don't you? I hope that goes well." Cherish hurried to the door. "Good luck with that, today, Debbie."

"She needs prayer, not luck." Levi held the front door open for Cherish.

"That's true. I'll pray about it as soon as I get into the car."

"Thanks, Cherish," Debbie said.

Then Cherish stepped out to the porch where Bliss and

the others were waiting. The driver took the suitcase from Cherish and closed it into the trunk.

Before she got in the car, Cherish turned around and saw Bliss's face. She looked so sad. Cherish whispered to her mother, "Can't we take Bliss too?"

"Does she want to come?" *Mamm* asked.

"I guess so."

"There's enough room in the car," Favor said.

"Well, ask her," *Mamm* said to Cherish.

Cherish turned around. "Bliss, do you want to come with us?"

Bliss's mouth fell open. "Can I?"

Mamm called out, "You can if you can pack your things in two minutes."

"I'll do it." Bliss hurried into the house.

Cherish was delighted and ran behind her. "I'll help."

"It's okay, I can do it."

Cherish remembered she hadn't said goodbye to Tommy and Timmy. She stopped and changed direction and headed to the birds.

She had Bliss looking after them, but now she was coming with them. Matthew walked up beside her. "Matthew, you'll have to look after the birds. Samuel will show you what to do. You have to be here every day."

"Every single day?"

"Yes. Will you do that please? Bliss was going to do it, but now she's coming with us."

"Okay."

"Thank you. Bye, Timmy and Tommy. I'll miss you." She put her hand in the cage and stroked each bird. Then she heard Bliss running back down the stairs.

"I'm ready," Bliss called out. "Oh, I can't go, Cherish."

"Why not?"

"The café. I'm taking your shift."

"It's only one shift. They'll be able to find someone else. Ask Levi to call them and tell them you won't be able to make it. They've got three days to find someone else. That's plenty of time."

"Okay." Bliss hurried out to talk with her father, then Cherish turned her attention to Matthew.

"Have you talked to Andrew yet?"

He rubbed his head. "Not yet."

Cherish huffed. "You've had ages to do it. It's been weeks since you agreed you'd do it."

"I will."

"When?"

"Um… very soon."

"Do it today." When he didn't say anything, she added, "Do you have anything else to do today?"

"No."

Samuel looked around the kitchen doorway. "Your mother's getting anxious."

"I'm coming right now. Matthew has agreed to look after the birds. Will you show him what to do?"

"Of course."

"I'll do it today, Cherish," Matthew whispered.

"Good." Cherish walked out, hoping she hadn't forgotten anything. Everyone was gathered on the porch and Cherish saw Bliss was already in the car, in the front seat.

"Be sure to look after Bliss. Don't ignore her," Levi said quietly as Cherish walked past him.

"I won't. I'm surprised she agreed to go. I thought she'd want to stay here in case Adam changes his mind."

"It's good that she's going," Ada whispered. "Try to keep her busy."

"Okay." After Cherish said a second goodbye to everyone and even said goodbye to the house, the horses, and the apple trees, she opened the back door to sit next to Wilma.

"I'm not sitting in the middle," Wilma said. "You go in the middle."

Wilma got out of the car so Cherish could get in. Cherish ended up being sandwiched between her mother and Favor. Now there was nowhere to put her head. Normally, on a long drive, she'd snuggle down and go to sleep. But, she couldn't complain too much because at least she was finally going back to the farm.

"I never thought so many of us would be going. We've left the house in the hands of Debbie and Levi."

"Ada will be around to help out. Matthew said he'd look after the birds and Samuel said the other day that he'd check on Caramel," Cherish said.

Bliss turned around. "Don't worry, *Mamm*. I'm sure everyone will be fine. Hope will be close by too if anyone needs a hand with anything."

An hour into the journey, Wilma told them, "I got a letter from Simon's parents the other day. They asked us to stop at their farm on the way. Since we drive through their town I said that we would."

Cherish grabbed hold of her mother's arm. "Wait. You got a letter from Simon's parents?"

SAMANTHA PRICE

"I did. I was leaving it for a surprise. Don't you like surprises?"

"No," Favor and Cherish said at the same time.

"How do they even know you?" asked Bliss.

"I've never met them, but when Ada found out I was going back to the farm, she called them and they reached out to me by letter. They have a phone in their barn like we do, so I called them and spoke to Harriet."

"You could've told me." Cherish looked down at the old clothes she was wearing. If she'd known she was going to meet Simon's parents today, she would've made more of an effort with her appearance. She might've even worn her new Sunday best that Florence had made.

"Oh, that'll be so boring. We'll have to sit in their stuffy house and be bored while you all talk nonsense about nothing in particular. We'll eat stale cake and drink lukewarm tea instead of hot tea. We don't even know these people," Favor said.

"We will know them after today. Besides, we know Simon, and his parents are good friends of Ada and Samuel."

Favor groaned. "Can't they just visit us at the farm like Cherish had already arranged? Why do we need to meet them before that? It's just a waste of time and it'll be dark when we get to the farm. I want to see all the animals."

"Hush," *Mamm* said. "It's all been arranged. So, you can be happy about it or suffer in silence. I don't care which."

Favor wasn't finished talking about it. "I'll just say this, I thought we were paying the driver by the hour. Visiting them will add to the time."

192

"We are, but we won't be there for long."

Cherish thought about it a little more. "I'm excited to meet Simon's parents. He keeps telling me how close he is with them."

Mamm said, "I guess that's what happens when you're an only child."

"I would like to have been an only child," Favor said.

"Thanks very much. What would happen to me then?" Cherish asked.

"You never would've been born. Aunt Dagmar would've left the farm to me, so your farm would be my farm."

"Or perhaps Florence's farm," Wilma said with a laugh. "Or was Florence not born either in your imaginings?"

"That's right. Just me. No siblings and no half siblings."

"Just lots of weird pen pals," Cherish added.

Favor opened her mouth in shock. "You're so mean."

"So are you. You're sad that I was born, and what about Bliss? Do you even want a stepsister at all?" Cherish asked.

Mamm raised her hand. "Stop this nonsense at once, girls. Is this what's going to happen at the farm? If it is, I'll bang both of your heads together to knock some sense into you."

Bliss sat in the front, saying nothing at all.

CHAPTER 32

ack in Lancaster County, Matthew tried to sneak out of his aunt's house. He was nervous about speaking to Adam's business partner, but he was more nervous thinking what Cherish would do if she found out he hadn't done what he'd promised.

He was halfway out the door, when he heard Aunt Ada's voice.

"What are you doing today, Matthew?"

He stopped and moved back inside and saw his aunt sitting by the fire, knitting. "I've got a free day. I'm not working at the saddlery store and I'm not starting at the orchard for several weeks."

She looked him up and down. "I heard you ask Samuel if you could borrow the buggy. Mind telling me where you're going?"

He looked down. "I can't really say."

"Sit!" Ada ordered, patting the chair next to her.

Reluctantly, he walked over and sat down.

"Now, tell me why you don't want to tell me anything. Does it involve a young lady, hmm?"

"Yes. Well, maybe, but not a young lady for me. A young lady for someone else."

Ada looked up at the ceiling. "So you're going to visit a young lady on behalf of someone else?"

"Not exactly."

Her head snapped around and her eyes bore through his. "Then what?"

"I'd rather not say." He had thought he could slip away unnoticed. She'd never been this interested in where he was going before today.

"What's the secrecy? I'm your aunt. You're nearly like my own son. If something's wrong. I should know about it."

Matthew shrugged his shoulders. If she kept going on like this, he'd have no choice but to tell her. "It's nothing that's wrong. It's just that I'm trying to do something to help some people."

"Some people, eh? Why would you involve yourself when it has nothing to do with you?"

"Because these are nice people and I feel someone has to do something to help." He was going to hold out, hoping she'd give up and let him go.

"Just tell me what it is, would you? Or would you rather sit here all day answering questions?"

Matthew swallowed hard. His aunt was never going to give up. "I was going over to Adam's workshop to see if—"

"You're trying to get them back together?" Ada grinned from ear-to-ear.

"If I can."

"What do you plan on saying to him?"

Matthew grunted. "All right. I might as well tell you the whole plan."

"You might as well and don't leave anything out." Ada put her knitting in her lap and leaned in close.

He told Ada of Cherish's plan for him to talk with Andrew to find out if Adam had ever made a mistake.

Ada rubbed her chin after she'd heard everything. "So what will you do if you arrive there and Andrew isn't alone?"

"My plan was to wait up the road and when I see Adam leaving, I'd go in and find some excuse to be there and I'd talk with Andrew."

"Cherish thought this up, did she?"

"Well, not me waiting up the road. The plan was to talk with Andrew. I thought about the waiting up the road bit. I know Adam is doing some work on jobs where he has to go and measure up. Like in Gertie's quilt store."

"That's interesting. I didn't know that. I'd say that would have to be Krystal's idea." Ada tapped on her chin.

"Exactly. That's what Cherish said. So if I find out Adam has made a mistake, Cherish wants me to tell her. Then she'll go to—"

Ada held up her hand. "I can see where this is going."

"Do you think it's a good idea?"

"It's a terrible idea. What Adam needs is to talk with his mother. All men need their mother's advice no matter how old they are. And, since his mother isn't around, I'll talk with him."

"You?"

"Exactly. Everyone says I remind them of their mother. I'm a motherly kind of woman—concerned and caring. You can drive me there. I don't like driving by myself anymore."

"Sure." The only thing Matthew could think about was how disappointed Cherish would be that he didn't follow her plan. And worse, that Ada had gotten the truth out of him. She'd never let him forget it. "Do you think talking with him would work? If I broke up with a girl, I wouldn't want to talk with my mother about it. I'd talk with a friend, or someone who's been through the same thing."

Ada stared at him. "You'd have to get a girl to agree to date you first before you talk to your mother about anything. Let's go. There's no time to waste."

Matthew was shocked at her comment. His aunt thought he had no hope of getting a girl to like him. Up until that moment, he had thought he was a pretty good catch.

Half an hour later, Ada and Matthew arrived at Adam's workshop. "You wait here in the buggy," Ada said as she stepped down.

Ada was focused on one thing only and that was to get Adam and Bliss back together. She walked into the workshop and saw Adam immediately and she called out to him and he turned around. Then he put down his tools and walked toward her.

"Morning, Ada. How are you?"

"I'm fine. I'm here to have a serious talk with you."

He raised his eyebrows. "About what?"

"You and Bliss."

Adam looked down. "Did Bliss send you?"

"No. That would be the last thing she'd do, but she is very upset."

"She's not the only one. There are things you probably don't know."

"I know everything. That is, if you're talking about the letters. Wilma tells me everything."

Adam looked over his shoulder. "Let's talk outside." He walked with her through the workshop and out a side door. Ada pulled her coat further around herself to keep out the cold.

Ada looked down at his bare arms. "Do you want to put on a coat?"

"No. I'm fine." He unrolled his long sleeves.

"What are you doing, Adam? You let Christmas go by and Bliss didn't hear a word from you."

"I thought about her. Of course I did. We were together for so long. Are you sure you know what happened, Ada?"

"I do."

He shook his head. "I'm not okay with it. I can't believe she'd deceive me like she did."

"But her mistake is not who she is. We all know that Bliss is a wonderful young woman. She's sweet and she's kind. She told me she kept writing to that man out of fear. Out of fear of losing you. That's how much she loves you, she feared losing you. And maybe this fear of hers led her to do that stupid thing."

"With respect, Ada, this has to be my decision. I've thought it through and I'm happy with my decision."

"And what is your decision?"

"To end things, which I have done."

SAMANTHA PRICE

"Would you reconsider? I mean, the girl's distraught. We're all so worried about her. Can't you just forget about the past and move on? You would still be with her if you didn't find out about it."

"She's not the Bliss I knew. She's not the woman I thought she was."

"We've all failed in one way or another. Who is without sin? Not one of us." Ada shook her head so much that her cheeks wobbled.

"That's a mistake that is not okay. Not with me. Some other man might be fine with it, but I'm not."

Ada didn't like how stubborn he was being. "I came here today because I thought you needed someone motherly to talk with. If you were my son, I'd tell you not to let Bliss get away. She loves you more than anyone else will. You two get along just fine. You're the perfect couple."

He nodded. "I can see how someone would think that. I thought that too, until I found out we weren't the perfect couple."

"But there is no perfect couple and there is no perfect woman. Can't you see that?"

"Thanks for coming to see me. I appreciate it, but my mind is made up."

Ada was shocked that her advice was falling on deaf ears. "Why are you being so hard-hearted?"

"Because I know myself. I know that what she did will always eat away at me. It's not only what she did, but the fact that she kept it from me. She only stopped writing to him because he stopped writing to her."

"Do you know that for certain?" Ada asked.

"That's what she told me."

"See? She was being honest with you. She's not a dishonest person."

"Too little too late. I do appreciate you coming out and pitching Bliss's case to me."

"We miss having you at the house too. Everyone does. It was like you were already part of the family."

"I know. I miss you all too, but that's just how things have to be for the moment."

Ada stepped closer to him. "For the moment? So there'll be a chance for you two in the future?"

"I didn't mean to imply that. Thanks for coming, Ada." He moved toward the door.

Ada stayed where she was. "Have you ever made a big mistake, Adam?"

"I'm sure I have. We all make mistakes."

"I want you to think about that." Ada gave a sharp nod and walked back through the building and then out to the waiting buggy.

"How did it go?" Matthew asked.

Ada shook her head. "It didn't go well."

"What did he say?"

"His mind is made up. Just take me back home, would you, Matthew?"

"Sure."

Ada was disappointed. She hadn't expected Adam to be so determined. Now she was concerned that she might have made things worse.

CHAPTER 33

*A*fter the third stop on the side of the road due to Favor being carsick, Wilma ordered Bliss to yield the front seat to Favor. The rest of the trip went smoothly, and Wilma and the girls finally arrived at Simon's parents' farm.

Wilma was the first one out of the car. She turned around and told the driver they'd be half an hour at the most. Cherish was still upset about her clothes, but she tried to put it out of her mind.

A short woman wearing a pale-green dress, that was longer than typical, came hurrying out with outstretched arms to meet them. She was smiling from ear to ear. "Wilma, I can't believe we've never met. Ada talks about you and your family all the time in her letters." She embraced Wilma. "I'm Harriet."

"I'm so pleased to meet you, Harriet. These are two of my girls, Cherish and Favor. This is Levi's daughter, Bliss."

"Pleased to meet you all. Come inside. Melvin and

Simon would've seen your car from the fields, so they'll be here shortly. I've been waiting anxiously."

They walked from the warm car, through the freezing cold, into the warm house. Cherish hurried to stand near the fire at the end of the room to keep warm.

Simon walked in through the back door, grinning. He took his hat off, smiled at Cherish and greeted everyone. Then his father followed. Simon introduced his father to everyone.

Cherish couldn't help noticing that Simon looked very much like his father.

When the adults were speaking among themselves, Simon spoke to Cherish, "I'm so pleased to see you."

"Thank you. I was surprised you left so suddenly."

"I make up my mind and then I have to do whatever it is. You know?"

"Not really. I think about how my actions will affect others." Cherish wasn't letting him off that easily for leaving without saying goodbye in person. A quick note in the mailbox wasn't good enough.

"We can't stay long," Wilma announced after Harriet invited them to stay for afternoon tea. "We have the driver waiting for us."

"It won't take long. Everything's ready in the kitchen."

They all moved to the kitchen and sat around the table.

Melvin said, "It's not often we get visitors. We haven't had many at all since we moved here. It's a nice change."

"Did you know we're going to the farm, Wilma?"

"Yes. Cherish mentioned that. We're only staying for six days. We'll be going home on Tuesday."

"We'll be there tomorrow, with Simon."

"Okay. That'll be fun."

"Simon and I will find some jobs to do on the farm."

Wilma laughed. "I think Simon and Cherish… well, the young folk might want to have some time alone."

"There'll be plenty of time for that, but I do like to keep busy." As Harriet cut the cake, she said, "I think the cake is still okay. I baked it last week."

Favor leaned forward and whispered to her mother. "I told you."

Wilma frowned at Favor.

"Simon tells me the farm is Cherish's," Melvin said.

"That's right," Wilma replied.

He scratched his head. "I've never heard of a woman owning a farm. Not someone so young either."

"Her aunt left it to her," Bliss said, speaking for the first time since they arrived.

Favor said, "And our aunt was a woman."

Melvin slowly nodded, "I guessed that."

Wilma frowned at Favor.

"When she marries, I guess she'll pass the farm over to her husband."

Wilma told him. "It's too far off to think about such things."

"It's nice that when Cherish moves to her farm that she and Simon will be so much closer," Harriet said, while Simon sat there in silence.

"Yes." Wilma was getting a little worried that Simon and his parents thought Simon was in some kind of relationship with Cherish. Had Cherish given Simon that impression? Was she in a relationship—a secret one? It would be just the kind of thing Cherish might do.

Harriet smiled at Cherish as she handed her a plate with a slice of cake. "I've always wanted a daughter, but a daughter-in-law might be just as good."

Cherish took the plate and then tried to cut the piece with a knife. Either the knife was very blunt or Simon's mother was a terrible baker.

"Could we take something out to the driver?" Bliss asked.

"He's welcome to join us," Melvin said.

"He will prefer to stay in the car. We've had the same driver before," Wilma said.

"Yes. Take something out to him. I'll pour him a cup of tea and you can put some of the cake onto a plate."

"Thank you."

When Bliss took the cake and tea out to the driver, he moved the window down and looked at it. "Is this the stale cake your sister was talking about?"

Bliss laughed. "Possibly."

"Nice of you to offer, but I brought my own food and a flask of coffee."

He nodded to a cup in the cupholder.

"You don't want it?" Bliss asked.

He shook his head. "Thanks anyway."

Bliss didn't know what to do. She didn't want to take it back to the house untouched. Just before she got back to the house, she tipped the tea into one of the bushes and buried the cake under some leaves. When she got back into the kitchen, she put the dishes into the sink.

"That was fast. He drank the tea and ate the cake already?"

Bliss froze. She wasn't thinking straight with the lack of sleep. "He was hungry. And thirsty."

Harriet raised her eyebrows. "Sit back down with us, Bliss."

Bliss sat down, hoping Simon's mother wouldn't find the cake in the garden later.

"Cherish, what do you think of Simon?" Harriet asked. A hush of silence fell over the room, except for Favor, who suddenly choked on her tea.

Cherish didn't know what to say. She looked at Simon, hoping he'd tell his mother to hush, but he just sat there. "He's lovely. Very nice."

"We think so. I'm glad you're so honest."

"There's no point in being any other way."

"My thoughts exactly. We'll get along just fine. Melvin and I are very close with Simon. You'll all find that out soon enough. We're more like friends than mother and son, and Melvin and he are more like friends too."

"Yes. He told me that," Cherish said.

"So, when he marries, that girl will be in a group of four with us. Instead, for now, it's a group of three friends," Melvin said.

Cherish couldn't work out what Simon's father was talking about. "Pardon me?"

"My wife and I are hoping Simon will marry a woman that can come into our group as a friend."

"What group?" Wilma asked.

"The friendship group that my husband and I have with Simon."

Cherish got it. "Oh."

"Do you like the sound of that?" Harriet stared at Cherish.

Cherish didn't like the sound of that at all and now she was starting to worry about Simon's parents coming to the farm. It would totally ruin everything. "I've got a great idea. We've got room in the car. Why don't we take Simon with us now and you can come when you arranged?"

"We don't have room," Bliss said. "There's already five of us in the car."

Harriet shook her head. "No. Simon wouldn't like that anyway. We like to go places together. When Simon went to your sister's wedding, it was the first time he'd been away from us since he was born."

"Really?" *Mamm* asked.

"That's right."

Cherish noticed her mother staring at the clock.

They left twenty minutes later when the driver knocked on the door reminding them of the time.

Once they were all back in the car, Cherish was relieved.

"Can you believe the things they were saying?" Favor asked.

"Shoosh. They'll hear you," *Mamm* waved politely as the car moved away.

"The only problem with Simon is his parents," Favor said. "They're acting like you're for sure going to marry Simon."

"Cherish," *Mamm* began, "have you been totally honest with me about your relationship with Simon?"

"I think so. I'm not sure what you mean. We're only friends."

"Hmm." *Mamm* didn't sound convinced.

"Will we only have one day on the farm before they arrive?" Favor asked.

"It seems like it," *Mamm* said.

"I wish I knew about this before I agreed to come." Favor folded her arms and glared at Cherish.

"I only invited Simon. Or did I? I'm not sure, but I can tell you for sure that I didn't invite his parents. They invited themselves. Maybe I did. I can't remember. I should've met them first before I did such a thing. If I did."

"It's all right," *Mamm* said, "we'll make the best of it."

"I thought they were lovely," said Bliss. "Simon has such lovely caring parents. He'll be a good father. He's had a good example of how to be loving."

"Loving or smothering?" Favor asked. "I was uncomfortable with what they were saying."

"They were only being honest," Bliss replied. "Bad things happen when people hide things. I learned that the hard way. I liked that they said what they had to say in front of everyone."

Cherish changed the subject so Bliss wouldn't dwell on her recent break-up. "I am looking forward to showing you the farm, Favor and Bliss. I think you'll both love it."

"I know I will just from what you've told me about it," Favor said.

Bliss added, "I'm looking forward to just getting away. Thanks for letting me come, *Mamm*. I know there's less people at home now."

"It'll all work out. Don't you worry, Bliss. Just enjoy yourself," *Mamm* said. "Ada is sure to help out. She always does."

Bliss nodded.

Cherish looked out the window thinking about how Simon just sat there while his parents said all those strange things—all in the space of several minutes.

What would their stay at her farm be like with Simon's parents?

Would Malachi mind that she was bringing so many people? All Malachi knew was that she was coming with her mother.

WHEN THE CAR stopped at Cherish's farm, Cherish jumped out first. She looked at the house and was pleased when the door opened and Malachi appeared. Her heart fluttered a little even though he was the same as always—totally disheveled. His hair was all over the place and the closer he got, she could see his clothes were all tattered and he was dreadfully untidy, and where was his hat?

Then she noticed a goose waddling behind him. Cherish opened her mouth in shock. "What's that, Malachi?" she shouted out.

He turned around and glanced at the goose. "That's Wally. He's the surprise I was telling you about."

"But... you don't like birds."

"He's not really a bird. He's a goose."

"Yes, but he's got wings and that makes him a bird."

Malachi shrugged his shoulders. "He's my new best

friend. He follows me everywhere. He was caught in one of the fences a few months back and I untangled him. He won't leave me."

Mamm got out of the car. "I hope you don't have the bird inside."

"I do. It's a goose," Malachi said.

"Leave him alone, *Mamm*. It's Malachi's house, at least for a while." Cherish grinned at him. Then she saw the smile fade from his face as he noticed the other two girls getting out of the car. "Oh, I forgot to tell you. This is Bliss and Favor. They've come too."

He smiled. "That's great. The more the merrier, I suppose."

Cherish knew she had to break the news about Simon and his parents coming tomorrow. "I also have something else to tell you." Malachi had walked over to help the driver get the bags out of the car.

"Malachi, we've heard so much about you," Favor said.

"I've heard about all of you too," he said, while he took two bags to the porch, with the goose waddling behind him.

Cherish pulled the two remaining bags out of the trunk and hurried to Malachi so she'd be the one to break the news.

He came toward her and took the bags from her. "I would've had the other rooms ready if I'd known."

"We can do that. I need to tell you something."

"What?" He kept walking.

"Stop and listen."

He stopped and put the suitcases on the ground and looked down at her. "I'm listening."

"We have some other people coming tomorrow."

Malachi folded his arms. "What people?"

"Simon Koppel and his parents."

Deep furrows appeared in his forehead. "Simon Koppel?"

"You know him?"

"I do." Malachi huffed and then looked down at the ground. "Do I have to stay here?"

This was worse than Cherish had imagined. Simon and Malachi didn't get along. "Of course. It's your house while you're living here."

"Not for the next week it seems. It's not surprising he's coming with his parents. They never let him out of their sight. And he doesn't seem too bothered by that, which is even stranger."

Cherish had to wonder once again, was Florence's husband right about Simon being a mama's boy? Surely that would change when Simon married, wouldn't it? Or, would he always do what his mother told him? "You're wrong about his parents. Simon came to Hope's wedding. He was the one I was telling you about that I thought was you from behind."

"Yeah, well you didn't tell me it was Simon Koppel. Are you and Simon…"

"No." Cherish shook her head vigorously as though that was the very last thing on her mind.

"So why's he coming here?"

"Well, he's just a friend. Like you and Annie are just friends."

He glanced over his shoulder at the barn. "You do what you want. I'll bunk in the barn with Wally."

"No, you can't do that."

"It's okay. I really don't mind."

"No. You'll freeze to death and *Mamm* won't allow it. The girls and I will sleep in one room and then there'll be plenty of room for everyone."

He shook his head. "I have to tell you I'm disappointed. I was looking forward to you coming. I wanted to have some time alone with you. Now that seems impossible."

"You wanted to have time with me?"

Malachi nodded. "I enjoy our talks."

"We can still talk."

"Come on, you two," *Mamm* yelled from the front door. "You'll catch your death of cold if you stay out there without coats."

Malachi picked up the suitcases and then they continued walking to the house with Wally close behind. Cherish hoped things wouldn't get out of hand this week with all the large personalities in one house. Add to that the fact it was winter and it could even snow, forcing everyone to be mostly confined indoors.

"Oh boy," Cherish said under her breath. "This could be the longest week of my life."

Thank you for reading A Season for Change.

THE NEXT IN THE SERIES

Book 26:

Amish Farm Mayhem

Find out what happens when some visitors join Cherish at her farm. You won't believe it! Cherish finally has a love interest but will she grow tired of his mother being the main woman in his life?

Along with a devastating natural disaster and the usual everyday disasters surrounding the sisters, this trip will be life-changing for one of the girls.

After much soul-searching, Adam finally makes a decision about Bliss.

A NOTE FROM SAMANTHA

I sincerely hoped you enjoyed A Season for Change. I had such fun writing this book. I can't wait to find out what you thought about it and I also would love to know what you'll think of the next book, Amish Farm Mayhem. So much happens when they get to the farm. It's my longest book in the series yet.
To chat with me and other readers, be sure to join my Facebook Readers' Group. I'd love to see you there.
https://www.facebook.com/groups/samanthapricereadersgroup

Blessings,

Samantha Price
www.SamanthaPriceAuthor.com

THE AMISH BONNET SISTERS

Book 11 Amish Apple Harvest

Book 12 Amish Mayhem

Book 13 The Cost of Lies

Book 14 Amish Winter of Hope

Book 15 A Baby for Joy

Book 16 The Amish Meddler

Book 17 The Unsuitable Amish Bride

Book 18 Her Amish Farm

Book 19 The Unsuitable Amish Wedding

Book 20 Her Amish Secret

Book 21 Amish Harvest Mayhem

Book 22 Amish Family Quilt

Book 23 Hope's Amish Wedding

Book 24 A Heart of Hope

Book 25 A Season for Change

Made in the USA
Middletown, DE
02 November 2023

41848423R00132